Adé

Adé

A Love Story

Rebecca Walker

Published by Little A, New York

www.apub.com

Amazon, the Amazon logo, and Little A are trademarks of Amazon.com, Inc., or its affiliates.

ISBN-13: 9781542047739
ISBN-10: 1542047730

Cover design by Gabrielle Bordwin

Printed in the United States of America

for Sefu
and all who love him

Yes, I know where that photo was taken. We have crossed that place together. There are fishing traps in the mangroves beneath the water.

— Adé

Adé

WE LIVED BY the sea, the two of us, many years ago, do you remember? We lived in a small green house that you painted every year after the rains. And in that house we made love almost every day and dreamed about all the lands we would see together, and in that house I imagined writing a book about being there with you. The book would be about love. I knew that then. It would be about living deliriously without all the things and people I held dear. I had you and I had the sea and I had the beautiful blue indigo the women wore on the cloths wrapped around their waists. I had fish and I had the taste of you — salty, musky amber.

OUR STORY, ADÉ'S AND MINE, began one afternoon in autumn. It was the kind of day New Englanders boast about, with red and orange leaves fluttering through an impossibly blue sky. I was walking with a friend, Miriam, down College Street. She was talking about sex with her new boyfriend and playing pinball at a bar on Adams Street. I pulled my coat tightly to my breasts and tilted my face toward the sun. And then the cavernous limestone gymnasium at the edge of campus was upon us, and we skimmed the wide, shallow steps until we were inside, enveloped by the gothic dark.

In the hushed dampness of the steam room, I reclined on the highest ledge, absolutely still on my towel. Miriam sat on the floor with her legs crossed, turning herself around in slow circles without a towel underneath her, her ample butt cheeks spread and rubbing against the faded green tile. She had huge pale pink nipples and smooth, fleshy thighs covered with hairs that made her legs appear tanned even in winter. She was like the zaftig women in the paintings by Ingres I was studying in my art-history courses, voluptuous women with skin like alabaster getting in and out of the bath.

"What about Thailand?" Miriam asked, so out of nowhere I thought she might be delusional. She began twirling faster. "What about Koh Samui and Phuket and Chiang Mai?" Spinning faster and faster, as if the words themselves were propelling her body.

"Mmm, hmm," I said, joining in. "What about Egypt? What about Karnak and Abu Simbel and Giza? What about Luxor and Aswan?"

"Yes!" Miriam said excitedly, going even faster now, no doubt chafing her buttocks and the backs of her thighs.

"What about the Nile?"

I was nineteen years old to Miriam's twenty-one. I felt raw and unfinished, where she seemed complete and self-assured. I was a child of divorce and felt like I came from a thousand places — each one holding a little piece of me, and I drifted among them with no way to gather them up. Miriam was from just one place, Miami, and more specifically, the moneyed enclave of Coconut Grove.

At Yale, she belonged to a set I had not known, even in the progressive environs of my gentrified Haight-Ashbury high school. Miriam and her friends built shrines to Madonna adorned with gold spray-paint and rose petals. They loved red wine and postmodern feminist artists like Cindy Sherman, Jenny Holzer, Frida Kahlo, and the Guerrilla Girls. They quoted Julia Kristeva, Karl Marx, and Simone de Beauvoir. They read Rilke and Thoreau and Whitman and nodded sagely when I brought a battered old copy of poems by Borges and added it to the makeshift library on the mantle of the old house that Miriam and her four closest friends rented on Howe Street.

I met Miriam in a film-studies class, Power and Politics: The Film of Latin America. We both wept at the end of the Cuban classic *Lucia*, and from that moment, were one. Together we limned the depths of normalcy, pushing the sharp edge of the envelope with our tongues. We crashed parties at elitist mausoleums and secret societies that still held the intoxicating perfume of luxury. We spent drunken evenings at Bar, the hangout of morose comp-lit students we loved to mock. We laughed over whiskey sours while they downed vodka and agonized over the anti-Semitism of deconstructionist Paul de Man.

I was fascinated by Miriam, as if she were an exquisite object, a multifaceted ruby, or a one-hundred-foot-tall Buddha. She paired a diamond ring her father gave her with a ripped polyester skirt bought at a thrift store for two dollars. She sometimes tied a colorful scarf over her dark brown hair and knotted it beneath her chin. She walked with her solid calves turned out slightly, as if she belonged to a village in the Old Country. When the neo-Gothic limestone of our Ivy League grew too much to bear, Miriam picked me up in her dusty red Chevy Nova, pink and orange strands of Mardi Gras beads dangling from her neck, and drove us out of New Haven to Cinema 21, several towns over. Some evenings we watched the sunset from East Rock, a tall bluff outside of town, interlacing our fingers and pressing our cheeks together to keep warm. Miriam was a force. She pursued, adored, and claimed me, and I was desperate to be claimed.

One day Miriam and I kissed, not because we felt passion for each other, but because we wanted to know what it felt like. We were on a ferry going to visit her mother. Our tongues collided as we left Mystic, with all its submarines and tools of war, and the Connecticut coastline trailing behind us. She felt strange and new in my arms, round and soft where my last boyfriend was tall and solid, moist and yielding where he was firm and sovereign. In that moment, I loved her more than all the rest. She was rooted but unbound. She functioned in the middle of the cacophony. I wanted to devour her and take some of her knowledge for myself.

One night not long after, the girls threw a rather large party, a soirée, at their house on Howe Street, and after too many bottles of wine and too much Bob Dylan and on the third go-round of Truffaut's *The 400 Hundred Blows* on the muted television set, I whispered to Miriam a little too loudly that I thought a boy across the room named Parker was cute — a little James Dean cum Jackson Pollock, very drunk and emotionally cut off, and thus, very manly. We were lazing on her huge bed, tucked into an alcove in the living room, by then; things were winding down, but many of the guests hung on. I wonder if he can fuck, I said to her as a kind of foreplay, and slowly reached my tongue to meet hers.

Miriam responded enthusiastically, to my kiss or the promise of Parker I can't be sure, but I accepted it willingly, just the same, with all the frisson of transgression. When we came up for air, the conversation had stopped all around us, and Miriam righted herself on her pillow, then filled the space with a throaty *Cat on a Hot Tin Roof* drawl. "Parker, Parker," she called, patting the mattress of her queen-size bed. "Come sit here, by us, honey."

It was a turning point, the first time we ensnared an outsider into our web, the first time we created an *us* that preyed upon a *them,* an *us* that, in loyalty and in every other way that mattered, took precedence over everyone and everything else.

Parker strutted over, beer in hand, cowboy boots clacking on the floor, and slid onto the bed alongside Miriam, kicking one leg over her already slightly parted thighs. In response, she ran her hand over his chest, casually unbuttoning his shirt and finding his nipples. He lurched forward and let out a low growl that made my own nipples stand up. Somewhere behind me I heard the tinkle of bottles and the rumblings of the exiting *salonistes*, but I was riveted by the scene before me, transfixed by what Miriam was creating for my pleasure.

That night we both had Parker, as many times as he would oblige us, and we kissed several times and rubbed each other's backs and thighs while Parker labored, reminding the other of the tender softness that was there too. But we never made love with each other, not in the conventional sense. There was no mounting or rubbing, no sharing of bodily fluids, though the intimacy of watching was intense. There was a moment so vivid — Miriam with her head back, her hand between her legs as Parker entered her — it could have been etched into my memory with a machete. She reached out her free hand to find mine, then opened her eyes and smiled at me, bridging for me the distance between beholder and beheld.

But then we wanted to sleep, and we wanted to do it without Parker. Suddenly he smelled bad and took up far too much room. We woke him up and told him to leave. He was hurt and looked it, even as his hangover bravado provided some cover. He pushed his face into his pillow, feigning exhaustion and mumbling about the cold, but we were unrelenting, verging on cruel. Finally, he pulled his shirt on, and Miriam slid close to me from behind. She draped her arm around my waist and I felt spent, delicious, and shockingly guilt-free.

At dinner the next night, over a bowl of pasta with mushrooms, Miriam exclaimed that boys could come and go — and here she raised her wine glass and leaned toward me, touching her perfect nose to mine. "But we," she said with a flourish, "we are what remains."

Within days, Miriam and I had a plan. We had traveled together before, but this time we would go for a year, maybe two. Within weeks a huge map of Africa was taped on top of the giant Walasse Ting poster of wildflowers hanging on the wall of my tiny off-campus apartment. As we drew lines and calculated distances, I eked out the last major paper of my college career on the poetics of space and the encoding of meaning into the built environment, paragraph by paragraph, citation by citation. There were days I thought I could not write another line, could not figure another way to make one idea tie coherently to the next. The giant map, the huge continent, beckoned, but Africa did not seem real. I could not imagine taming the beast at the computer.

But then one day, there it was. The end. Miriam and some friends took me out for tapas. I ate olives, little pieces of bread dipped in oil, a salad of tomato and fish. I drank wine, a nice Sancerre. I came back to the apartment afterward, light-headed, and began to pack. I threw hundreds of pages of drafts into a huge black garbage bag and tied it shut. I sat in the middle of the living room, watching the sun come up, as Segovia played classical guitar through the tiny speaker on my windowsill.

Miriam came to check on me in the early afternoon. We rented a storage space on Orange Street, and she had picked up the key. We took our books over, and the chair and ottoman splashed with green flowers I bought for twenty-five dollars at the Salvation Army. My paintings — a Mexican girl standing by the window, the Picasso etching my father gave me as a child, a huge disfigured ghost I bought from an art-school student who buried his canvases for months, then dug them up as if reclaiming dead ancestors — went too, encased in large cardboard picture boxes. I kept my favorite sweater and unceremoniously dumped the rest of my clothes on the porch of the campus ministry. I was spent and hungry, high on the promise of the unknown.

And then we left that place, the cold walls of stone. We were going. We were in flight. We were gone.

FOR THE FIRST few weeks of travel, it was as if I had been asleep for a thousand years. I had been all over America, but hadn't yet seen the bridges of Prague, the arches at Auschwitz, the ports of Gorée. I hadn't walked the streets of Paris at night, or wandered the enormous Buddhas at Angkor. I hadn't sipped water from the Chalice Well at the foot of Glastonbury Tor, or gawked at the Harajuku girls in Tokyo. All of these places live in me now, many years later, but then, before I met Adé, when I was still a child, my body was almost clean, like a plain piece of cloth without tapestry, batik, or indigo. It was as if nothing penetrated until I began making my way toward him. And then it was as if I had been dying of emptiness, so readily did the world bleed into me.

We landed in Cairo and moved south. Following the date palms? The desert? The hidden voices of all the women I couldn't see? Or was Adé calling me, in silent prayer, as he rolled up his fishing nets? Whatever it was, I made my way to Giza — or *Gi-ʒeh*, as the women and men who lived there called it, spitting the word to the ground from full dusty lips. In Giza I wandered past the pyramids and the Sphinx and the Kentucky

Fried Chicken shop directly across, out of the parched, gravelly earth and into the verdant valley, the emerald-green fields dotted with ancient palms. I arrived with Miriam, but found that in Giza I wanted to be alone, to blend in with people who looked like me, and so I left her in the compound where we had taken a room, her fleshy white calves tossed over the lip of an enormous washtub in the courtyard, her slender fingers reaching for a bottle of shampoo we had bought in Tahrir Square.

"I'll be back," I said gently.

She kissed me on the cheek. "Bring chocolate. Please?"

In Giza I carried a camera as a crutch for conversation: *Can I take your picture?* followed by *What is your name?* and *Do you live here?* My Arabic was poor and yet the women and children, and sometimes the men, talked to me, standing with their arms wrapped around faded wooden posts, staring at the way I dressed, the way I walked, the way I pointed the camera at them. A few times I was invited in for mint tea, and I accepted, passing shyly into living rooms of pressed earth, bare but for a rug caked with dirt, a fire pit with tin pots stacked off to the side. The tea was brewed from fistfuls of the herb pressed into a blackened, fat-bellied kettle, sweetened by mounds upon mounds of brownish sugar poured from wrinkled sacks.

I know for many reasons that it is unfair, exploitive, and blasphemous to think this, but I began to feel at home there, walking between the palms, looking at the pink and purple, turquoise and orange clothes, faded but clean, fluttering on gray clotheslines crisscrossing above me. Some might say it was only First World romanticism causing me to see myself reflected in the faces of those to whom I could not speak. And yet at each house, even though I had no words to tie us together, a recognition between me and my hosts rose up and hung in the air, roping us together long after I had walked away.

As night fell, I rode the buses in Giza and other outlying suburbs of Cairo, making my way on rickety old trolleys that ran from Tahrir Square to Maadi before returning to the perfume and parchment hawkers at the Sphinx, where tourists of every nationality swarmed like the flies we swatted from our plates at dinner. On the buses I was overtaken by children, tens of them in blue and white school uniforms, chattering loud and fast to one another, thrusting their heads and arms and fingers outside the gaping holes that served as windows. After a lifetime of being the only copper-colored girl with brown eyes the shape of almonds, I was now one in a great mass of long lost reflections of myself. The language was different but the skin, the way we looked moving through the colors and contours of the world, was the same.

The women gazed at me intently, without reservation, their dark eyes boring holes into the side of my face. I imagined their thoughts. What kind of a person was I? What was I doing in their midst? Was I their sister? What would I tell them? That Miriam and I had a vision to see their place while sitting in a steam room across the world? Certainly I could not tell them what I did not know, that I was finding a new home, shedding a self that made me foreign. That I was, in fact, being reborn before their eyes.

"*As-salamu alaykum,*" I said to their stares.

"*Alaykum salaam,*" they answered respectfully, before looking away.

After weeks of this, so many that I kept time by the muezzin's call to prayer, Miriam and I decided to leave the city and head south to see the temples of Abu Simbel guarded by enormous statues of Ramses and his queen Nefertari, saved from the Aswan Dam by Jacqueline Onassis. We wanted to meet the Nuba people of Sudan even farther south, the huge men Leni Riefenstahl captured in washed-out black-and-white photographs, virile as gods, carrying one another on their shoulders.

I knew we would also find war and famine in the Sudan, and shitty towns with only syrupy soda to drink and goat meat swimming in fatty broth to eat, but still I wanted to go. Even when people told me I could die there in the desert — be kidnapped, murdered, or worse, raped, I persisted, disbelieving. It did not occur to me that I could be hurt, or that anything could be bigger or stronger than my own will to move freely, unobstructed, across the plains. Perhaps this was because my parents had divorced when I was very young, and left a fault line in my psyche. I was accustomed to the shaking of the earth. I knew it was inevitable, unavoidable — it was how things would always be. I was not afraid to fall between the cracks.

In Aswan, I dared to swim in the Nile even though there was said to be giardia in the water. I ignored the young men who manned the felucca and told me with emphatic, agitated gestures that the current of the Nile was deceptively strong; I could easily be carried away, past the tomb of Aga Khan and over the perfectly smooth boulders that lay in the eddies like sentinels. I nodded, but knew that I had to submerge myself, to feel the cool brown green of that mighty river against my skin. As if possessed, I threw one leg over the side and then the other, and then I was in and swimming and imagining all of my illnesses, each and every one of my impurities, being washed away.

The Nile was a baptism, an initiation. All the elements were there: the water, the boat, the young men named Mohamed and Amir and Hassan gracefully managing their flowing robes, balancing barefoot on the prow of the dhow. The meals with them at sunset, the breaking of the fast with dates and beans made with onion and tomato that appeared miraculously from beneath worn strips of foil on cracked and faded plates. They tolerated me, a foreigner, a stranger, with a rough tenderness as they would a sister, or a wild girl from another place, or maybe more realistically a brother, pulling my heavy, waterlogged body from the water, handing me huge chunks of bread dripping with fava beans; in Arabic, *ful*.

In the end I was struck down only by the heat, the piercing and relentless quality of it, the absence of shade by the rocks. Because there was water all around I did not feel the need to drink it. Because they offered it, I did not question the food I was given. I lost and then regained consciousness. When the doctor came with needles and hydration packets, I willingly extended my arm, my feverishly hot body undeterred. When he reached under my blouse to see if women from the West were as promiscuous as advertised, I vomited on the pale blue bib of his shirt.

At the border, dark men with AK-47s slung over their shoulders forbade us to enter Sudan, so we climbed back on the bus back to Cairo, and made it back just in time for the train to Sharm el-Sheikh, a tiny dot at the tip of the Sinai. As was my habit by then, I struck up a conversation with a woman on the train. She took mercy on us when I told her where we were going, and begged us to look for a tea shop run by a woman named Mouna.

"The Sinai is very big, and very empty. She will help you young girls. You must find her. Mouna, you will remember that name, yes?"

After the train, we hailed a taxi and asked the driver to let us off close to the shop, but he knew nothing of it and dropped us instead in the middle of nowhere. We tumbled onto the famously embattled triangle of land that Israel always wanted but Egypt would never cede. The air was black and cold; we could barely see each other. A building that might have been a bus station was closed, and any passengers long gone. We combed our guidebook by flashlight until a young soldier stopped his jeep alongside us, appraising the two women sitting, perfectly balanced, on their backpacks. He asked why we were alone. He asked if we needed a place to stay. He told us his name, Mustafa. He barely looked at Miriam but said I reminded him of his sister. At his compound, he gave us chunks of feta cheese, a piece of bread, and his narrow bottom bunk for our weary bodies.

In the morning, the sky burned with the blinding desert sun. We splashed cold water on our faces, and Mustafa pointed to a crop of purplish mountains outside of the one window in the military dormitory.

"There, there is Mount Sinai, where Moses received the Ten Commandments," he said. And then he turned his body the other way and gestured to an endless stretch of sand. "And there, there, is where they will build the hotels." He moved his arm a bit to the left, gesturing toward another dusty brown strip. "And there is where the road will be, a big wide road." His fingers scraped around an orange he had pulled from the refrigerator, peeling it, and he said, "This is the place where all of the tourists will come.

They will come from all over the world to this faraway, crazy place. Then we will know the war with Israel is over, and we have won."

Miriam and I looked at him, this handsome young Egyptian of sharp nose, full lips, and dark eyes framed by lush lashes as long as any woman's. His pronouncements seemed preposterous. The train station was two hours away. We were eating *beans* from a can in the communal kitchen of the only standing structure visible in any direction. Even now, in broad daylight, there was nothing to see.

"Come, come. You do not believe? You do not believe? I will show you." He dragged us out of the building, him pulling Miriam and Miriam pulling me, and took us to the edge of the cliff we found ourselves perched upon. "There," he said. "Do you see all of that water?"

We looked out over the Arabian Sea with its azure waters and large swaths of shallow green revealing the silky white sand beneath. "There are hundreds, thousands, of fish out there," Mustafa said. "They will come, you will see, the tourists, for their scuba and their snorkel and all of that, you will see, and this place will be like Israel's famous Eilat."

He spat on the ground and then looked directly at me. "But everything for Egyptians. Egypt for Egyptians. You know what I am saying, don't you? Everything for us this time." And he told me again. "Ah, you look like my sister, you know? Her name is Fatima."

Angling for inclusion, Miriam used some of her newly acquired Arabic. *"Fein?"* But Mustafa ignored her completely.

I said we were in Sharm to find Mouna's shop. "Do you know it? Mouna's?"

"*Aiwa,* of course I know Mouna's. We go now?"

Miriam and I looked at each other. It occurred to both of us then — she looking Israeli, me feeling Egyptian — that something about us would never, could never, change. Without my saying a word, I was being drawn, compelled, to the other side of a line. I felt less and less like an outsider, and more like someone fated to be in this new place. To stand where I stood. Miriam could not enter with me, not fully. She could only watch.

The tent rose up from a vast plain of desert in the middle of the Sinai mountain range surrounded by nothing but sand, a bunch of white flaps fluttering in the wind. A dozen ten-year-old Mercedes-Benz sedans were parked neatly out front. The cars were identical: cream colored and completely covered in the constantly swirling dust that coated everything in Sharm el-Sheikh, with brightly colored pieces of carpet gracing each dashboard.

In Cairo, men had gestured angrily until we fled the tearooms, hands covering our heads, shuffling through cross-legged patrons, painfully aware of our womanhood. But Mouna's was filled with men drinking tea, smoking hookahs, playing backgammon, and singing verses along with the ecstatic incantations of Oum Kalthoum (*"The Voice of Egypt! The Fourth Pyramid!"*) that streamed from tinny speakers powered by a long line of extension cords. Mouna appeared from behind a curtain leading to the backroom a few moments after we entered. She clapped and sang loudly along with Kalthoum, her arms reaching up, up, up, lifting the energy of her patrons. She was not covered. She was the first woman I had seen in public who was not wearing any part of the hijab. Her face was bright and her body full, with hips that swayed to the music. This woman was not afraid. She was not a stereotype. It occurred to me that this place, Egypt, and perhaps the rest of the Islamic world, was unpredictable.

Mouna headed straight to me, her arms outstretched. *"Habibi!"* she exclaimed. Darling! "Where have you been all of this time?" And then my face was buried in her bosom, and even though I was confused and overwhelmed by the instant familiarity, I wanted to stay there, enjoying her ripe smell and ample warmth. Her solidity.

"I have been away," I said, finally disentangling myself, not comprehending my own response. I looked at Miriam quickly, as if to say, *We're good on this, right?* She beamed, approving, loving the idea of being inside, across the line, even vicariously. "I have been in *Amrika,*" I went on. "But I am home now."

We stayed with Mouna for a month, listening to her story, washing tea glasses and serving customers, learning the names of her Bedouin regulars and listening to their lives. Mouna's family disowned her when she announced she would not be wearing the hijab, nor marrying the man they had chosen. She roamed the streets of Alexandria alone, the city where she was born, continually subjected to taunts, until one day she slipped unseen onto a train, and then a bus, and arrived at Sharm determined to live her own life. Hassan, a tall, silent Bedouin we met a few days after our arrival, took her in, and eventually gave her the money to open the tea shop.

"And today we are known all the way to Alex!" Mouna said, beaming. "My family cannot bother me anymore. I make my own money. I run my own business. That is it, isn't it? This is what we are supposed to do, is it not true?"

I wanted to record Mouna's story as proof of something. The tenacity of the human spirit, or a woman's escape, or maybe I just wanted to take part of her with me. I couldn't imagine leaving her there in the middle of that desolate expanse, surrounded, yes, by men who loved her, but fundamentally alone — with no other women around to mirror her courage, her breathtaking will to thrive. Miriam didn't feel the same longing, and by then had made her own friends, men who liked to watch her dance and who shouted uproariously each time she beat them in backgammon. In the afternoon, she often visited a few of their wives; they braided her hair, and she taught them to write their names in English.

The night before we left, Hassan and Mouna arranged a farewell feast in the desert. Miriam and I were forbidden to take part in the preparations. Mouna said we were to be treated like royalty. For what reason, we could hardly say. For arriving at the teashop? Recognizing Mouna? Validating her life choice? For whatever reason, Mouna made sure every detail was polished to perfection, and told us we would not have to lift even one piece of bread except to eat it.

"It is a party for you, my sisters," she said, "something we will remember until we are finished with this life."

One Mercedes was filled with a goat, red wine, and plates of tomato, cucumber, hummus, and lemons. Another was filled with barefoot children who ran to us at the last minute, arms loaded with firewood, laughing with excitement in their embroidered *galabiyas*. The first Mercedes, which would lead the others, was for the four of us. Miriam sat in front with Hassan, and Mouna sat in the back with me, holding my hand. It was the beginning of our goodbyes. She was orchestrating a farewell with no tears, no bitter herbs — only sweetness.

Hassan started the car, and we headed toward the setting sun. I had become accustomed to driving in the desert. That is to say, when Hassan led the three-car caravan, I didn't look for a road because I knew none existed. I had learned that the Bedouins knew this triangle of land like they knew their own names. I didn't understand it — how they could drive for hours, day or night, and arrive at their destination without a road compass or landmark of any kind — but I discovered that my lack of understanding was irrelevant. They could and they did, as if the whole of the place, the entire land mass, was a huge, three-dimensional grid inside their heads, a map imprinted at birth.

A few hours after sunset, Hassan abruptly stopped the car. Again, I saw only miles of nothing, but carpets were unrolled and a fire was made. Miraculously, a goat was cooked and people began to play music on small instruments pulled from their pockets. A small boy took my hand and led me to the reason we had stopped at this place — a wadi, a large pool of water, a mirage that wasn't a mirage — and he motioned for me to sit down. I saw the crescent moon reflected in the water, and gasped. He laughed. "*Amar*," he said, pointing to the moon. "*Nejma*," he said, pointing to the stars, of which there were millions, lighting up the sky like the tiny phosphorescence that danced around me when I swam in the sea months later with Adé, laughing at the magic of the tiny bits of aquatic fire. I nodded and repeated the words back to him: *amar, nejma*.

I tried to read his body, from his soft brown eyes and faded *galabiya* to his long, tapered fingers and the way he sat on his

knees, palms turned up on his thighs. My patient instructor would
be a man someday, but tonight he was a boy translating the uni-
verse, giving me his world with his words.

On our way back to Cairo, Miriam and I stopped for a few days in
Dahab, the place of gold, before the flight to Nairobi, and rented
a square cement room with two mats on the floor for fifty cents
a night. When the sun rose and the morning was still cool, we
rode camels and gazed across the water at Saudi Arabia. I spent
the sweltering afternoons in the shade, talking to old men under
baobab trees who called me *mok kabir*, big mind, as I cajoled them
into teaching me more words. Sun. Water. Rain. *Shams. Ma.
Mathar.* One man asked why I wanted to know so many words.
He was tall and dark, a luminous black figure with long arms and
legs, sitting erect on a sun-bleached white stone bench.

"So I can talk to you, and you can tell me things," I said.

So I can truly be here, I thought. So I can become of this place,
and not the other.

After Dahab, we flew to the relatively crowded streets of Nairobi
and went into a kind of shock. We were in a real city again; the
tall office buildings and sidewalks full of expats and Kenyan busi-
nessmen in boxy suits threw us. We scrambled to the other side
of town and secured a cheap hotel where, in an altered state and
apropos of nothing but an inner call to metamorphosis, I started
hacking at the long, thick ropes of my hair with a pair of rusty
scissors I found on the sink.

It was hot and swarms of mosquitoes made their way through
the screens on the windows. I was changing. I was becoming
someone else; I was emptying myself of identity. I wanted to give

all of it away, everything I had, and everyone I was. Miriam hovered as I snipped, making sure I only thinned the great mass I had grown for a decade, rather than shearing it off completely. She kept telling me not to move too quickly, as if she sensed I could shock myself out of self-recognition. That I could get lost and not find my way back.

We quickly had enough of the metropolis, the young hustlers and prostitutes, the piles of garbage, the incessant sounds of the *matatus*— privately owned minibuses — rounding up their passengers. Foreboding posters of President Moi, Kenya's brutal dictator well into his second decade of power, were plastered everywhere: the exterior walls of every business, the front door of every home, the base of every monument at the center of every roundabout. A traveler at the airport with a backpack three times the size of ours had mentioned the islands off the coast of East Africa ringed by white sand, and we decided to go, to get back to where we could breathe.

We came to the decision lightly, like all the others. There were signs, but it was also intuitive, something bigger, this way we followed another calling. In the morning we boarded an ancient bus headed to the coastal town of Malindi. From there we would take the ferry to Adé's island of sand and stone — his speck in the middle of the Indian Ocean, Lamu.

WE STEPPED OFF the bus with our backs kinked and mouths dry. The twists and turns of the road from the city to the coast, the loud yelling of the bus driver and his obvious addiction to an herb pulled obsessively from a wrapper of old newspaper had left us skittish and raw. The other passengers did not seem to notice the careening into darkness, the hypnotic beat of imported hip-hop pumping through the threadbare seats, the angry outbursts of passing motorists.

Miriam and I tried to let our bodies sway with each lean and brake, tried not to conjure images of mangled bodies and buses overturned by the side of the road, but found we could not help ourselves. We sat the whole sixteen hours clutching metal bars crudely nailed into the sides of our seats, rivers of sweat streaming from our armpits. We glanced meekly from time to time at our fellow passengers, men and women who awoke from naps refreshed and took pity on us, offering cigarettes and bottles of hot cola as we quaked.

To finally climb aboard the ferry that took us away from the mainland of Kenya was to step into a dream. We were never so glad to leave tar and cement, metal and glass, profane music and men who did not take precautions. The boat was not big, but it was old and looked to us seaworthy, though of course there would have been nothing to do had it been otherwise. It was painted white and a calming pale green, and once it began to move, groaning loudly as the waters churned beneath us, it did not take long for the coastline to disappear, and for the fumes and chaos of the dock to fade from view.

I was worn out, but had never seen a swamp before, and certainly not the vivid mossy green of mangrove forests, the bent reddish-brown trunks rising up out of the muck, miraculous as lotus blossoms. Again, I felt a sense of belonging — the slow, irrational dissolution of the self I had known, and another, core truth of being emerging in concert with the landscape. I wanted to know about the small islands we were passing. Were they inhabited, did food grow there? But I knew better than to talk to the women cloaked in black and laughing insouciantly at their own jokes, wrapping and rewrapping their coverings while staring nakedly at me as if I were no more than a life-size cutout of a woman, and not the real thing. I sensed there was a code to this place, and that I knew it. I did not believe in the notion of a return to the homeland — such an Africa was gone, I knew that, and yet, there was something akin to a homecoming. As in Tahrir Square and Maadi and Gizeh and Sharm el-Sheikh, I felt familiarity in my marrow.

Those moments of being watched on the boat were another kind of initiation — the women cut me into pieces and then put me back together again. I felt the burn of their stares acutely. But there was nothing to be done, no one else to be. My role was to be quiet, to make myself as still as possible while continuing to hold my body in a way that seemed normal. I was being apprehended and to speak would have been to thwart the process, to deny these women the chance to run me through their filters, to digest me and, therefore, let me inside and I knew that inside was where I wanted to be; that I would be accepted in the eye at the center of the storm, and so I calmed myself and let myself be pulled across the divide.

Soon the landmass appeared on the horizon, and then all at once we were upon the tiny village, a string of flat, tin-roofed buildings, and the boat was roped to the hooks on the cement pier by a barefoot man old enough to be my grandfather. I noticed the Portuguese influence, the squat columned structures reminiscent of the slave trade, but it was not my first thought, nor did it take hold for long. I was already caught up in what was going on around me.

It was mango season, and mangoes were everywhere: loose and spoiling on the ground at my feet, carried in bulging sacks on the backs of men, bright orange and dripping in the hands of children along the sea front. Women were covered from head to toe in black, strolling unhurriedly in groups of four and five. Young, shirtless men with dreadlocks and surfboards were scanning the ferry passengers for rich white tourists. Older men in neat white shirts and embroidered skullcaps were walking briskly to and from mosques that dotted the small town.

I don't remember how we got from the pier to the guesthouse, but our bags were tossed onto the concrete, and we were escorted from the mouth of the boat onto the firm ground of the pier. Miriam and I stood there for a few moments amidst the orderly confusion, too tired to check the guidebook buried in our baggage and too happy standing still to rush to movement. Then a young, brown-skinned man with thick-rimmed black glasses approached us with a mixture of boredom and pity, picked up our bags with-out a word, and led us through the narrow, winding streets to our new home, a few tiny rooms off a rooftop courtyard, completely hidden from the street but for a narrow stone staircase winding up from the curb.

Adé did not appear until many hours later, after the sun had melted into the sea and the sticky heat of the day had settled into a breezy cool. I had unpacked the contents of my bag into an old wooden chest that stood beside the thin mattress on the floor, and hung my brightly colored scarves on hooks pounded into the cracked, dry walls. The sheet on my bed was faded and flowery, and I stretched out on top of it in the dimly lit room, hearing the muezzin's call to prayer and thumbing through a book of poems, *The Captain's Verses*, by Pablo Neruda. The tightness in my neck and in the small of my back relaxed, and my mind began slow-ing to the pace of the island, downshifting from the screeching city chaos to the gentle lapping of the sea that beat like a pulse through the tiny town.

Gradually the opening and closing of doors and the shifting of furniture outside my door grew into laughter and talking and the sound of food and drink being served. It was Ramadan; the sun had gone down, and the music had begun to play. That night the fast was broken with a melodic Lingala, and I immediately put my book down and let my head fall back into my pillow. I had not heard Lingala music before, and the newness of the sound af-fected me. I was used to the haunting whines of the griots from Mali and Senegal, the polyrhythmic chants of pygmies from Cen-tral Africa. But Lingala was different. It was music born of Af-rican rumba, a child of Afro-Cuban fusion that took hold in the

Belgian Congo in the forties, and made its way east to Kenya and Tanzania in the seventies and eighties, absorbing influences from Congolese folk music and Caribbean and Latin beats. On the Kenyan coast it leapt again, and with three or four guitars, one bass, drums, brass, and vocals, evolved a new offspring, benga, or the Swahili sound. Lingala was dance music, hypnotic and polyphonic, full of movement. It brought to mind the sound of bottles tinkling at a bar, and women and men sweating and dancing hip to hip under colored lights. The sound was so infectious, so sexy, it drew me out of my room and into the movement of it, into the ecstasy of its freedom.

I opened the door, and saw a man in the center of this exuberant stream of sound. He was inside the benga. Standing with his back to me, among a dozen or so other strikingly beautiful bodies, I saw his slender hips first, the clean white *kikoi* wrapped neatly around his waist, the tails of the turquoise button-down Oxford shirt modestly covering his behind. Adé's was the first body I saw, and then my eyes were captivated by others: a handsome African American man I later learned was from Boston, a thin, olive-skinned beauty from Brazil, a serious exchange student from Tunis, five or six diffident looking young men from the island. Everyone was talking, drinking, laughing, and sharing survival stories from months on the road.

Miriam had already found her station among the celebrants, stretched out on a beat-up sofa, holding court, no doubt sizing up which man she might bed. By now I was used to her insatiable appetite, the way men fell at her feet, mesmerized. She felt me looking at her, turned and caught my eye, and motioned for me to come and sit. I walked to her slowly, and from my new perch turned to look for him, the man at the center of the sound, the first man I noticed, but he had already gone. And then I felt silly, who was I to him? I had only opened my door and found him standing there. I had no right to summon him. But he was at the center of it all. He was all I saw. I wanted him to come back and stand with me. I wanted to see his face. Instead, I lay my head on Miriam's shoulder as she ran her fingers through my hair and pressed my cheek further into her sturdy frame.

Adé returned only after the bottles had been emptied and the benga tapes had been played again and again. Miriam had disappeared, but I knew she would return soon, it was only the first night, after all. I was stretched out on a wooden chaise, with a towel wrapped around my legs to protect me from the cool of night, when I saw him at the top of the staircase. He had changed into a different *kikoi* and T-shirt. His hair was carefully combed, and his hands and feet glowed clean. He carried a Styrofoam plate in one hand and in the other, an orange Fanta. I said hello and we looked at each other, and then he said how are you and I said okay and he asked if he could sit near to me to break the fast. I said I would not mind at all; in fact, it would be nice to have some company because everyone else had gone to bed.

I sat up and told him my name, offered my hand. His hands were full, so he bowed his head respectfully and told me his. Adé. "What does that mean . . ." I asked. "Ah," he said. "It is not important, I have some time to live up to this name. But it is to mean royal, the one who wears, how do you call it? The crown. It is not a traditional Swahili name," he said. "My mother gave it to me because she thought I should be like a lion." "King," I said, laughing. "Yes." He smiled sheepishly. "But it is a long way off, no? I have much to learn."

I made room for his solid six-foot frame on the chaise, taking in his broad shoulders and strong arms as he gracefully brought the plate and bottle of soda to rest. We did not touch — he was careful not to come too close — but the power of his physical presence moved me. He, it, radiated an honesty that was unfamiliar, a blend of humility and self-awareness, confidence and modesty all at once, and when he turned to face me, I gasped a little at his unselfconscious beauty. I saw his dark eyes and full mouth, his sharp cheekbones and clear, brown skin, and then, of course, the totality of him — all the parts put together.

I collected myself and asked where he'd been. He told me he had gone to the mosque to pray. For four hours? I exclaimed, smiling, warm but skeptical, having long ago been trained to distrust religion. No, no, he said laughing, that would be too much. Only for a little while, he said, but before that he had to clean and shut down his dhow, bathe, and visit with his mother. Every evening during Ramadan he visited her, he said, to talk over the day's events outside her small house.

I asked if this was customary, if all the young men on the island went home to their mothers in the evenings during Ramadan. He said that some did, but not all, and then I was quiet and thought of all the stereotypes I had of Muslim men. I had not imagined them spending hours with their mothers. He told me that when he sat with his mother, he also gave her the money he earned each day, and they discussed how she would use it to manage the house and feed and clothe his brothers and sisters. I had never known a man to bring home all of his earnings, to hand the fruits of his labor, a fistful of cash, to his mother, his wife, his sister. To a woman.

Out of habit — I was trained at university, after all, to pose questions such as these — I asked if his mother was allowed to work, if she ever had her own money. And then I worried suddenly that I had crossed an invisible boundary.

But no. After a beat, Adé looked at me and said, "But my money is her money. My mother," he said, "she works very hard. I wish I could give her even more." I felt both ashamed and put at ease. His calm openness in the face of my implicit criticism seemed the better way to move in the world. I exhaled and looked past him at the moon rising, huge and luminous behind us, from the other side of the island. I motioned to it and he twisted around to see. We stayed like that for what seemed a long time, watching its ascent in silence.

Eventually he turned back to me and asked if I was hungry. I was not, but again, just as with the women in the boat, something stopped me from responding as I might have, loudly and without respect for the sanctity of the moment. I said yes quietly, almost in a whisper, and watched him carefully take the thin sheet of tin off of the plate. As I parted my lips and waited for the forkful of noodles he offered, I glanced at his muscular calves, and his large and handsome feet resting in sandals made from the faded black rubber of old tires. And then the spaghetti reached my tongue. It was sweet! It was cooked with sugar! It was one of his mother's favorite recipes, he said. It was special for Ramadan and meant to remind us of the sweetness of life, of God.

I nodded, pondering this new being before me, feeding me the taste of his mother's hands, her offering to God, and I had the urge to touch him, to feel that he was real. And then the sweet spaghetti was finished, and he said he had to work early the next morning at the woodshop. He was a fisherman first, but also a carver, he said, and chiseled rosettes into the massive wooden doors announcing the thresholds of the larger houses in town.

We had seen some of them, I said, on our way to the guesthouse. He nodded. I wanted to kiss him, waited. He folded the square of tinfoil covering the plate and put it into his shirt pocket. I stood closer to him, and we walked together to the steps. He was taller than me by several inches, and I felt some indescribable protection there, in his imagined embrace.

After he left, I lay on my thin mattress, thinking about the unusual potency of our attraction. I knew nothing about him and yet I wanted to see him again. I had too much power, I thought. I might consume him out of my own curiosity simply because I could. I could stay or go. He could not. He had too much power, I thought. He could reject me. He could break me in two.

Not long after, I heard a quiet knock on the door and for a moment thought he might have returned. But it was Miriam who entered without waiting for my response. She spread out next to me, humming a tune from the Lingala, as I gushed excitedly about the moon and the sweet spaghetti, about young men giving money to their mothers. She talked about the invisibility of women in the old town, and the claustrophobia she felt walking down the narrow stone streets. She said that for the first time in her life, she missed seeing cars, a way out.

I tried to stay awake, but was tired and did not like what she was saying. I could not imagine we were on the same island. I started to say something, to defend this small place and its people, but I could not bring myself to do it. I had only just met this one boy. The story of the world was too big to reverse in one night. My mind and then my body grew heavy. I pressed myself against her, and drifted off to sleep.

WHEN I TOLD my mother I wanted to travel to Africa for a year, maybe more, she did not flinch. She thought it an excellent idea. She had traveled to Africa, too, when she was a few years older than me, and written her first book of many, a collection of poems, inspired by the experience. On the appointed day of departure, we stood in her study, in front of her typewriter, and she wrote me a check for three thousand dollars. She smiled as she handed it to me, happy, I think, to have the means to give me the gift of another continent. Then we hugged, which gave the exchange a ceremonial air. A seal of approval, a nod of expectation of what was to come: discovery, expansion, and, of course, art.

Africa was part of our mythology. We talked about African novelists like the South African writer Bessie Head, who went insane. We met the Ghanaian literary star Ama Ata Aidoo when we traveled to London. Shona marble sculptures from Zimbabwe graced our home, along with gorgeous books about the Ndebele people who paint their houses in brightly colored, abstract designs. My mother bought enormous photographs of pygmies from Zaire, and hung them, with their great round bellies and expressive eyes, in the living room. When the opportunity arose, she made sure I met Nelson Mandela, and a photograph of the three of us, smiling, was perpetually on display.

In our house and in our relationship, Africa was not foreign, threatening, or exotic. It was inspirational, full of powerful people with tremendous intellects who made remarkable contributions. Africa was a rich and looming place and my mother made me feel, through her words and actions, that it belonged to me. It held secrets, she said to me in her own, quiet way. Things I would never hear if I did not go myself.

My father was altogether different. He nodded gravely when I told him where I was going, and arranged for me to have my own American Express card added to his account. He didn't appear concerned about the trip itself, but that it included Miriam seemed to chafe. In the months before we left, Miriam sold me her car, and he didn't find it roadworthy. His younger brother had been killed in a car accident while driving home from veterinary school a decade earlier. For my father, it was a defining moment.

We were living in Washington at the time of the crash; my father was working as an attorney in the administration. He woke me up in the middle of the night and carried me to our sturdy Volvo for the long drive to New York. We sat shiva at my grandmother's house in Brighton Beach, and I watched in horror as the headstrong woman who never finished high school, worked several jobs as a bookkeeper, and bought me wildly decadent things like gold-plated jacks, wailed and beat her chest. Some days she could barely stand, or bring herself to look at the people filing through her tiny living room to pay respect.

At night she clutched my father's lapels, demanding, "Why, why, why?"

He held her and looked into her eyes as his own filled with tears. "I don't know, Mama, I don't know."

My father, the rock of each family he coalesced — with my mother, with his mother, with the mother of my half-brother and sister — told me he worried every time I drove "that car of Miriam's." I drove too fast, he said, and he was right. I hated the monotony of the road, especially the stretch of highway from New Haven to his house in the suburbs of New York City, and I was young and arrogant enough to think poorly of all the other drivers. I deemed them slow and too focused on the road. I was more interested in the destination. The accelerator in Miriam's car was also smooth, too smooth. What took other drivers two and a half hours, I accomplished in two, sometimes less.

One night before Miriam and I left the continent, I slid the car up to the front of the house and saw my father though the living-room window, waiting quietly, reading Reinhold Niebuhr. He looked up from his book, stood and walked outside, ambling down the cement path from porch to curb. He hugged me, kissed my forehead, and then commenced his ritual inspection of the car.

"Dad," I said impatiently, "the car is fine. It's fantastic. Stop worrying."

He checked the tires, crouched to see if any fluids were dripping from the machine's underbelly. "I don't like you driving this car, sweetheart. It's not safe. I don't see how Miriam's parents let her drive it. And now you're going to another country with her?" He shook his head in resignation, then put his arms around my shoulders, steering me back to the house, toward safety.

My sister ran to greet me as we came through the door, giddily wrapping her four-year-old arms around my legs, and shouting my name.

We sat for two hours in the wingback chairs, and I listened to my father talk about my brother's success in little league, and the musical talent he must have inherited from my great-grandfather.

"You know," he said, "your great-grandfather was a composer before he lost his sight and opened the newspaper stand on Fifty-seventh Street."

I nodded. He had told me this a thousand times.

"Yes," he said. "He lost his sight in the small-pox epidemic. You must always be careful, my oldest daughter," and this last he said with gravitas, "You never know how this life will unfold."

He was right about everything, of course, but I was already gone. His house, his stories, his tragedies, could not hold me. I did not see them as my own. He was locked in his past. I was hungry for my future. It looked painfully bright.

AFTER THE SWEET spaghetti, on those last days of Ramadan, Adé came after the sun went down and took me for long walks through the old town, a place full of movement during the day, and absolutely, eerily still at night. On our fourth or fifth walk, we held hands, our fingers separating only when I had to lift the hem of my sarong to keep it from trailing into one of the many reeking puddles of liquid — water, donkey urine, who knew what else — at every curb, or when Adé pointed at a place significant to him, a landmark on his road of his life. The doors he carved for a powerful man in town, the tea shop his cousin owned, the site of the old hospital long torn down.

A few weeks after Ramadan, we walked to the seafront and sat on the low wall of stones at the edge, staring out at the moon. We were quiet, holding hands in the dark, until he spoke. "I don't know how to say this," he said. "It is something that makes me uncomfortable, something not easy but I know I must tell you, or I will always be holding it in my mind, and that is not fair, to keep secrets between each other. Even though we do not know each other very long, we know each other in the right way, and that is something you cannot measure in normal time.

"It is that I have feelings for you. Or? I can't say exactly, it is that I am always thinking of you. When I am working I am thinking about coming to see you, or walking in the night with you, like this." He paused and looked out at the water. "Do you think I should not say these things? Maybe I should keep them only to myself, but you are something different, or isn't it? Look at you, you are more Swahili than a Swahili girl, you are respectful, not like the others who come. My stepfather tells me to be careful, but to him I say the world is big, the life is long, who am I to say no to you just because you are not born on Lamu?"

I was quiet. I had already fallen in love with his words. For whatever reason — his halting dance with my language, his tender heart — when I listened to him, I heard the tremulous vulnerability of poetry. He had split me open weeks ago.

Before I could speak he continued, "I know you will say that it will hurt too much when you leave, that we should stay only friends, but there is a saying," he said. "*Kipendacho moyo ni dawa.* I am not sure how to say in English, but it is like, how do you say, What the heart desires is medicine to itself. Does that make sense?"

"What the heart desires is medicine to itself," I repeated back to him.

"Yes," I said, wondering how I would ever, in a million years, leave this man.

"Yes, yes. That makes sense."

A few weeks later, Adé told me I needed a new name. "You need an Arabic name," he said, looking at me carefully across an old backgammon board we discovered in a corner of the guesthouse. We were sitting at a table on the rooftop in the heat, a few dozen feet outside the door to my little room. The call to prayer was a low whine straining through the sticky, hot damp of impending rain. I looked at him, slid a worn brown circle across the elongated triangles on the board, and laughed into his eyes.

"Really?"

We had taken to meeting on the rooftop during the day because something happened when we walked the narrow stone streets in the light. People stared at us, studied our movements, and murmured about our togetherness. Shopkeepers, fishermen, men mixing cement. Women who slid by so quickly I didn't know they took us in until they had already turned away. The community was small, yes. But also, I had come to find out, Adé was well known in his place, on his small island. Respected. Walking with a woman in public, an *mzungu,* a foreigner, meant something about him, about me. People, his people, were waiting to see what.

"I think Farida suits you," he said, pausing with the import of the moment before picking up the dice. "It means the woman who is exceptional, a jewel. There is no other like her. She stands alone."

I smiled.

"But this name, will your father mind? It is a real Muslim name."

We had been speaking of religion. The night before I explained I was not brought up in any formal religion, but my mother was born Christian and my father, Jewish. He had turned his head quickly to face me when I told him this.

"Really? Your father is *Judeo?*" He laughed, showing his dazzling white teeth. "This we cannot tell my mother yet."

I had raised my eyebrows, anticipating one of the long, sometimes contentious discussions we had been having about religion and culture, the winding talks that alternately clarified and vexed, but then, finally, brought us back to each other with a newfound understanding: his view of America was partial and tinged with propaganda; my feminist view of Islam was phobic and left no room for gray.

"No, no," he said. "It is no problem, but she will be shocked to know I like a Jewish girl. She wants me to marry a traditional Swahili girl I have known all my life, but now I do not think that is the life I want for myself."

"What is the life you want for yourself?"

"Ahh, I don't know, I am young, I don't know my destiny yet," he had said, as if his life was something to be revealed to him at a certain age, in a particular moment.

"I don't think my father will mind," I said now, wondering about my own destiny. "I will just have to explain it to him." And then I laughed out loud at the thought of sitting with my father in his office on Madison Avenue. I would translate my new Arabic name while perched on one of the sofas we had picked out together at Bloomingdale's, when I insisted he needed furniture in the office where he spent most of his life but none of his money.

A sketch of him arguing in the Supreme Court would be on the wall to my left. If it was after five o'clock in the afternoon, the blinds covering the windows on one side of the corner office would be lowered to keep the setting sun from hurting our eyes, but the other bank of windows would remain open to the fading light. I would look out between the hulking gray buildings of concrete and steel, beyond the thousand tiny boxes of light, each filled with a legal assistant or advertising executive sitting behind a desk, to catch a glimpse of the liquid path of the East River.

I would tell my father my Arabic name was Farida, and he would laugh and laugh from behind his L-shaped mahogany desk, leaning back in his armchair, eyes twinkling.

"You are amazing," he would say. "You travel to the other side of the world and come home not with little tchotchkes from the tourist shop, but with a new name and a Muslim mother-in-law!"

Then we would laugh together, because he was right, it was ludicrous. We would not speak of the underlying currents. My nomadism was legendary, a label slapped onto a deeper childhood fracture best left unspoken: the collapse of our home, our family, the brutal ripping apart of my foundation. My classmates were applying for prestigious grants and law schools. They were like trains, each on their own track forged in steel. I envied their certainty. But I was first-generation Ivy League, only the second generation in my family to go to college. My genes were new to this place of privilege. I felt lost on campus, but the dislocation was deeper than that. It rumbled through generations.

"But wait," I said to Adé, snapping back to the present, my tongue heavy in my mouth. I knew the importance of naming in his culture. "Are you trying to tell me something? Am I to be always alone? Are you saying you don't want me — that I must go and live by myself? That I am not your future?"

"What is the meaning of this? This, Farida?"

Adé looked at me quizzically, and then reached across the small table to take my face in his hands. He said that was not at all what he meant. But he had never met a woman so independent and so beautiful, so full of ideas and open at the same time. And then he leaned in and kissed me with lips so full and so warm, I felt a rush of heat flood my body and then only desire. I pulled him from his chair, kissing him all the way through the door of my room, and then I was pulling him to the floor, down onto my thin mattress, over me, on top of me, heavy, new, hard, wanting.

I led him through the steps of lovemaking, either because he did not know them or his nervousness had gotten the better of him. I coaxed him, massaged his neck and whispered my new name into his ear as he entered me. His climax was almost immediate. I didn't mind. Drops of rain began to fall, and I held him in my arms like a child, even though his body was big, bigger than any man I had ever loved.

After, he told me I was his first lover.

"I have never done that before," he said, looking up at me, his face as open as the sky. "You are my first love."

And then, "You will be my only love."

I looked at him, at his sparkling, smiling eyes, and felt the foreign becoming familiar. I was beginning to feel at home in another land. He gave his mother all of his money every night. He fed me sweet spaghetti. He gave me a name. He answered all my questions about Islam and everything else with unwavering patience. He rubbed my feet at night. He covered the vein that ran down the underside of my arm with soft, tender kisses. I was to be his only love.

Who was I to say we were not each other's destiny?

I told Miriam the next morning. She shook her head and began pacing the worn, colorful rug on the floor of her small room. She became animated and emphatic the way she'd been in the steam room months before, spinning.

"Don't get attached. It is dangerous to get attached."

In a great rush of words, she said she was ready to leave the island. She found the tourists annoying, the Muslim men disrespectful. She said the place wasn't real. It wasn't really Africa. She was bored.

"We have to get out of this place," she said, digging through her life-size backpack propped against the wall. "It is just a fantasy land for rich Italians. This girl I met, Sarah, says all the men just want to find a woman from the West to pay for them to travel to Europe or America. It's not real. None of this is real! How do you not see that, you of all people?"

She pulled out her notebook, the threadbare blue rectangle she carried with her everywhere. Receipts and little scraps of paper with names and phone numbers scrawled across them in her left-handed script bloomed from its edges.

"I met a guy with a glass factory near Lake Turkana in the north," she said, unsnapping the hair band holding the notebook together. "It's supposed to be amazing. There's an overnight train through the blue hills, and then a twenty-four-hour bus ride north. From there we can go west to Uganda. There is a ferry across Lake Victoria."

She was still pacing.

The idea of a twenty-four-hour bus ride followed by a ferry to anywhere made me want to run screaming from the room. I did not want to move again, I did not want another place to slip through my fingers. I did not want to get back on the never-ending train of my life. For once I longed to arrive, not depart.

After a few more moments of listening to her plans, I finally stopped her. "Is the man you met from Turkana more real than the men here?" She stopped, midstride. "What is the difference between here and there, really?" I said. "Why run from this place? There is time. It is safe."

Her eyes — hazel, green, blue, they changed with the sun — stared into me, screaming astonishment and heartbreak. We were supposed to travel the continent, to pass through places, not become part of them. I was breaking the covenant, betraying the map.

"Well, to start," she said, her voice now tinged with sarcasm, "there are no tourists, and only a hundred or so people in the whole village. He invited us to stay at his mother's house."

I waited for her to continue.

"Oh, and it's not a beach town full of boy prostitutes looking for sugar mommies."

The blow. She was talking about Adé, and she was talking about her idea of the "real Africa." My stomach jumped in rebellion, but I found I didn't have the words or energy to explain. I wanted to tell her that she was chasing a myth from the pages of *National Geographic,* that she had read too much Paul Bowles, that she believed in some kind of impossible contrivance of purity. I wanted to tell her I had never subscribed to the idea of a "real Africa" to begin with. I wanted to tell her I was sorry that I wanted to stay, that I had found a place and it was becoming a part of my history.

Perhaps I should have said all of that, but at the moment I did not have what it would take to build that bridge; the burden of crossing the divide was, even for her, for us, too much to bear. How to tell the entirety of my life in a way she could understand?

A glimpse of the future passed wordlessly between us.

"I don't want to go to Lake Turkana," I said gently. "I want to stay here and read the African novels I've been lugging everywhere. *The Beautyful Ones Are Not Yet Born* is as long as *Anna Karenina*. I want to read it in one place, sink into it. I want to write. I want to learn how to cook coconut rice. Here."

And then I said what we both already knew. "I want to stay with Adé."

She looked up at me, reaching for common ground, but I saw jealousy in her eyes. She was usually the one to meet a boy. Wherever we went, men wanted her. Her breasts were large, her mouth willing. Even I had wanted her, but that part was over between us. We had moved on from our infatuation to the meat of things: men.

As I listened to her plead, and talk about the smell of sewage in the street and donkey shit on the sidewalk, I saw the balance of power shifting. I had always followed her, but here, now, it was becoming clear: I would not be seduced by her pursuit. I had become the beacon of my own desire.

Perhaps the seed of our separation had been planted weeks earlier, I thought then, in Sharm el-Sheikh, in Mustafa's glimmer of recognition. *"Ah, you look like my sister, you know?"* Miriam, the Israeli, and I, the Egyptian. We did not know how to talk about it, but we felt it, and now there was this, this bush between us that could, at any moment, go up in flames. In her room, I felt the shrub beginning to burn, I could feel the heat, and I took pity on her. I didn't say what we were both thinking: I belonged here, and she did not. And so I released her, the only way I knew how. I took her hand, kissed her cheek, and told her what she needed, but did not want, to hear.

"You go."

She nodded as her shoulders slumped in defeat, and fell back onto her bed. She knew she could not fight me. She knew I didn't need more. She knew I could fall in love on this island and stay. As for me, well, Miriam was no longer enough. She was seaworthy, but Adé was the sea itself. She had Coconut Grove. She could always go back home. I was never sure if the homes I left would be there when I returned. The Indian Ocean was stable; the moon rose up out of the water like a planet. Adé knew how to navigate it by the stars.

I hugged her, and when I looked back from the doorway, she was sitting on the small bed, clutching her blue notebook. She looked bewildered. Betrayed. I felt guilt but lacked doubt. This new world — with its Afro-Arab-Portuguese inhabitants with whom I shared bone structure and skin color, and whose brown eyes appraised me as if they knew me better than I knew myself — had claimed me in a way I had not known. The island was becoming my home. My mother's prophecy was becoming manifest.

NOT LONG AFTER the first night we made love Adé brought me to meet his mother. She lived in a small clay house with a fire pit for cooking in front, and a hole in the ground in the back for everything else. Her mother, Adé's *nyanya,* spent most of the day lying on a cot in the short, narrow hallway that served as both living and dining room.

The day he took me, holding my hand, telling me it would be okay, Nuru Badi was sitting outside her house in the spot I would come to know as hers, because I would soon greet her there on the many days and nights I came to visit. At first, I did not understand her pride of place, but then I grew to admire her strategy. From her chosen perch she could watch her children — the smaller ones from her current husband — and also keep an eye on the fire burning beneath the huge aluminum pot filled with coconut rice and vegetables for the evening meal. Her long view included the paths that brought her sons and husband back to her at the end of each day, and the position of her chair, slightly turned toward the road, allowed her to keep track of all the other comings and goings of her realm.

Nervously, I greeted her in the way Adé had taught me, kneeling before her and saying the appropriate words, *Shikamoo Mama*. To say she appraised me the way all Swahili women did would be to understate her response. Nuru stared at me, straight into my pupils, and held my gaze as she spoke to Adé. I knew enough Swahili by then to understand most of her words.

"Who is this girl, Adé, and why are you bringing her here? What is the meaning of this?"

This is Farida, he said gently. I told you about her, do you remember? We met during Ramadan.

"She is *Amerikani?*"

Yes.

"What part does she come from?"

From New York. It is a big city, much bigger even than Nairobi.

"How old is she?"

She is still young, Mama, you can see for yourself.

"Where did you meet her?"

At the guesthouse. She is new here, with no family, only one friend, another girl.

"Doesn't she have parents who are worried about her traveling so far from home?"

Things are different in America. Her parents want her to know the world is bigger than just one place. And she has already been to university. She is not a child.

And then the final question:

"When is she leaving?"

Which is when Adé surprised me by saying what some small part of me had been thinking but not dared say aloud.

She is not leaving.

And then Nuru Badi cracked a smile, mostly with her eyes, and waved me in to meet her mother.

I began to spend whole days at Nuru's house, cooking with her, making her laugh at my feeble attempts to wash clothes. I could not wash everything with just three small cups of water. She could, and I watched her at least a dozen times as I tried to figure out the science of apportioning the small amount of liquid just so, but I found it impossible to duplicate her formula and was reduced to caricature. The water spilled. I forgot to keep some separate to do the rinsing. I put the clothes down on the dirty ground when they grew tangled and heavy.

"*Eh we!*" Nuru would scold me, the words snapping from her small mouth. "Don't you know Aliyah had to go all the way to Ngomani for this water? Do I have to send her again? It is a long way for a little girl, you know."

Nuru was stern, but she told me stories about Adé when he was a boy, how he slid out of her body in just a few minutes, eyes wide open. She told me the meaning of her name: "beautiful light," which made sense. Her face was round and golden brown, her black eyes sharp and bright. She poked cruel fun at me too. Each time her sisters came over and tossed aside their voluminous yards of black cloth to reveal their pretty floral dresses and voluptuous figures hidden underneath, Nuru told them a different story about my profound incompetence.

Her best son, her most faithful, her smartest, her hardest working son, had brought her a useless daughter-in-law, she said. I couldn't cook or wash clothes. I couldn't even make a proper fire. They all laughed, clapping their hands and shaking their heads, tearing up at the absurdity that was me. I wrapped my *kanga*, the patterned sarong I bought in the market, tighter around my waist and pulled my scarf over my head to claim what dignity I could muster until Adé came to save me.

"Stop making fun of her," he said. "She is not from here. She does not know the ways of this place. You should be ashamed, Asha. Was it so long ago that you were afraid to even take the boat alone to the mainland? And that is just a short distance, not even one half hour! Farida has traveled across the world on an airplane for more than twenty hours — do you hear me? Be patient with her, she will learn."

The sisters looked down, but not Nuru. She held her eyes up, taunting us. "Here, here then, my grown son," she said, rising from her stool and walking into the tiny, narrow bedroom, "take these shirts your future wife has washed!" And she showed him the clothes I had wrestled with for hours, with the streaks of dirt still visible around the seams, and the soap barely rinsed from the cotton.

I wanted to cry, but Adé took the shirts and motioned for us to go. He flipped the shirts wordlessly over his shoulder as we walked the crooked stone streets back to the guesthouse. After a few minutes of silence, he reassured me softly, "My mother is not really angry. It is her way of testing us. She is trying to make sure you are strong, that you will not leave me at the first sign of trouble."

As the days passed, I grew used to spending my days waiting for him. I would shower, letting the lukewarm water from the communal stall on the rooftop rinse me clean in the morning. Then I read a hundred pages or so of one of the African novels I found at the kiosk or bought off of a traveler passing through. I wrote in my journal. I sketched in the book of unlined pages Adé brought to me one evening. "Why not draw?" he said. "You are always taking *pichas,* isn't it? Maybe some should come from inside. Not everything can be found from looking out."

On some days I took grocery orders from Nuru and walked to the market for fruits and chapatis, or a packet of pencils for Adé's youngest sister; other days I made my way to the sea, all the way to the end of the beach, where the women sat cloaked in black. I'd sit with them, not speaking, looking out at the ocean, and trying to get a glimpse of Adé in his dhow, wondering how he was managing under the hot sun.

One evening Adé said he had a surprise for me. He had something to show me. He said he had been working on it in secret for weeks, but wouldn't tell me what it was. He clasped my hand and led me from my rooftop down to the cobblestone streets, and then took me higher and higher above the old town, stopping every now and then for air. When I looked up at him, pleading and impatient, he told me to keep going.

"Patience, Farida! We are almost there, you will see." But the suspense was excruciating. I imagined we might be going to visit his older sister, Amina, and her husband. Adé told me they were having a hard time; the husband was cruel to her, and though I asked several times, Adé refused to take me to their house.

"He is very rich, and he is not our relative," Adé had said. "It is not the right thing to do, to go to him. Amina must come to me first, or I cannot help her."

I had met Amina once, at their mother's house. She was standing behind a high-backed wooden chair, holding it as if to shield her from any perceived threat. She was stunning, the epitome of all that was revered in her culture: creamy, light brown skin; dancing, dark brown eyes; a thin, perfect nose; straight, white teeth.

She was slim, with modest but seductive curves not fully revealed even in the dresses she wore underneath her floor length covering, her *buibui*. She was present, but quiet, almost invisible.

I smiled at her tentatively, as if approaching a rare bird. She smiled back, and I immediately felt transported to another house, another room, another land where the light of the equator streamed through the windows like the northern light in a Vermeer. I understood immediately why Amina had been snapped up by a man so much older, a man of means. She would be day to his impending night.

Finally, Adé and I came upon a small, newer house. It was clean, bright white, but still in the old style: smooth stone, elegant arches, and a large tub of water with a cup for a shower. I didn't get the meaning until we climbed to the top floor and stood on the terrace overlooking the island — the old town to the left and the white sand of Shela Beach spreading to the tip of the blue-green Indian Ocean to the right. I clutched Adé's hand tighter. He had found a terrace for us, far from the hustle and bustle below, a vantage point for us alone. I saw myself in a chair, legs outstretched, my journal in my lap.

"There is more," he said. "I am not sure you will like it, but it is a beginning. It is for now until we can make something better. Come."

He led me to a low doorway a few steps back from the terrace. Another structure was perched atop the building. He pulled a key from his pocket — I had never seen him use a key — and opened

the tiny door. It was a room, a room for us. A bed stood in the
center of the small space; he walked me over to it and placed my
hand on the headboard, the dark wood carved with a single, exquisite rose.

"I made this bed for us," he said. "For us to sleep, for you to
read and write. Maybe, who knows, we will make a child in this
bed." I looked around. The room was almost in miniature, with
only two small windows, the bed, and a small table. A few hooks
for clothes. A hot plate. The mere idea of a breeze.

Then he gave me the same big smile as he did after the first
time we made love. "Let us get married, Farida. This is only the
first step. I will build a house for you. And we will have children,
and you will learn everything. I promise."

What could I say? In the logic of our unfolding, it made
perfect sense. The days had turned into weeks, the weeks into
months. It could not go on open-ended this way, not in this culture. If we married I could stay forever. I would have a permanent home, as unchanging as the thousand-year-old stone streets.
I would be free to leave, but always expected to return. I would
learn how to wash clothes and cook delicious food over a fire.
I would learn all the things I did not know about the island. I
would never have to survive another cold winter, in a cold city.
I would write a book. I would have children. I would be happy. I
would give up everything and gain even more. I saw it all.

Yes, I said, a young girl full of idealism. Of course it was possible. Wasn't it? Why couldn't Adé be my future? *Ndyo. Kabisa.*
We will be married. And I tilted my face up to his as I had done,
by now, so many times, waiting for his lips to push against mine.
And we fell onto the creaking but sturdy bed, the both of us

laughing about its potential to hold our weight, and made his gift our own.

Later, as Adé walked me back to the guesthouse, he took my hand in such a way that I could tell something powerful had shifted. His hand felt bigger, more possessive, certain.

"We will go and call your parents tomorrow," he said. "It is Saturday, so I don't have to work on the dhow. We will not tell them yet, my parents should hear first, but yours should know you are safe. I will wait in line with you at the post office."

I nodded, thinking about how much my mother would approve of Adé, his careful inquiries and overriding gentleness. I would tell her that I was thinking about staying longer, for weeks, months, perhaps a year. I would tell her that I felt at home in Africa. That I was receiving the message I was meant to hear.

The next morning Adé and I walked together down to the post office situated at the water's edge, and while waiting in line for the phone, we watched the ferry dropping off and picking up passengers and supplies. The dock was teeming with men heaving sacks filled with everything the island could not create: rice, wheat, sugar, textiles, and tea. We were there early because it was still relatively cool; the sun had not yet become hot enough to drive us indoors until the late afternoon, when it would be bearable again to walk the narrow, car-free, streets.

An hour plodded by and then it was our turn. Adé negotiated the rate with the man behind the counter, arranging as always for everything to be less expensive for us. If the sunburned tourists loaded with backpacks and guidebooks had to pay three dollars a minute to call home and were only allowed five minutes, we paid fifty cents and talked however long we liked. Which is what we did, ignoring the stares of others who had been waiting in the heat, on the hard bench. It could not be helped; I had to tell my mother everything: Adé, his mother, my rooftop, and the brightly colored *kangas* I now wore draped over my head or around my hips.

"They have sayings printed on them!" I said. "The one I am wearing today says *Haraka, haraka, hakuna baraka* which means, if you are in a hurry, you won't get the blessing."

My mother laughed her big laugh when I told her this, and Adé did too, his ear pressed against the receiver listening for the sound of her, the living place of my birth. I began to feel like an intruder standing between them, keeping one from the other, and so I passed the ancient handset to Adé, who took to it like fire, his voice softening with respect. *"Jambo Mama."*

His face grew serious as he listened to her with unflinching sobriety. "All is well," he said, utterly appropriate for the moment. "Do not worry. I know she is far from home, but I am taking care of her. Even my mother, she is taking care of her."

This last utterance made me feel like a little girl wearing a little yellow dress and standing only to Adé's kneecaps. I fought an urge to skip and jump up and down. He was taking care of me. Even his mother was taking care of me. I was being slung over a warm hip for the rest of eternity.

Adé handed the phone back to me and I was an adult again, but softer, more vulnerable this time.

"He sounds so tender," my mother said. "I'm so happy for you. This is good."

I nodded my head. "Yes," I said. "Yes, this is good." And my mother and I laughed conspiratorially. I was meant to replicate her experience, but at the same time remake it to fit my own life. I was still constructing our mother-daughter house, but Adé and his island were pillars supporting the whole.

Before leaving the post office, Adé and the man behind the counter exchanged a few parting words, implicit with promise of future favors, reciprocity. I reveled in these moments. I was so used to taking care of myself, of quickly surmising the lay of the land and negotiating it for survival, that the sheer ease of it, of having to do nothing at all, flooded my brain like a drug.

I knew from that day forward, the man from the post office would not look me in the eye because it would be a sign of disrespect. If we passed each other one afternoon on my way to the storefront where I bought passion-fruit juice, he would nod deferentially, eyes lowered, telegraphing the silent knowing of my position. I was part of Adé's family now. I was spoken for. I commanded the same respect as his sisters or cousins. The blend of anonymity and acknowledgment was exquisite. I was free, but protected.

I was alone, but never without the specter of my man.

Within the week I told Hassan of our engagement, and bid him, the proprietor of the guesthouse in which I had lived for so many weeks, a teary farewell. I moved my books and clothes into the new room, our first house, and immediately set about making the place our own. I swept the floor and covered the bed with a large white *kikoi*. The cotton was thicker than the cotton of the *kangas*, more like soft canvas than muslin. I hung my wraps on the hooks, adding streams of color: bright orange, pale blue, a rich, loamy brown. I arranged my collection of novels, spines out, in a neat line along the floor. I collected fruit — mangoes mostly, but also passion fruit and guava — in a bowl by the bed. I gathered chalk-white stones from the beach and lay them in a mound on the tiny bedside table. I bought amber musk from one of the scent shops and sprinkled it in each corner of the room.

Adé did everything else. He bought the extension cords necessary to light the coils of the hot plate. At night he cooked my favorite foods: coconut rice and *mchicha,* a spinach-like leafy green. Mango soup. He hung the mosquito net over our bed. He showed me a dozen times how to shower with the tin cup and tub of water and scolded me, jokingly, about my inability to use water sparingly. He washed all of our clothes, quickly and efficiently, and hung them on a retractable line he strung across the terrace.

One day I went out with him on the dhow and an unexpected shift of the tide left us stranded on another island in the archipelago. The next day I could barely move — my entire body was on fire from what the sun had wrought — and Adé walked the island for hours until he found a local remedy, then laid me gingerly on our bed and slathered the concoction in smooth, even strokes across my back and down my legs.

As the days passed, we spoke Swahili and English, him looking up from the tiny outdoor washbasin, his face streaming with water, eyes half closed. *How do you say?* And he would point to my toothbrush, his leg, or the loaf of bread on the tiny table. *Mswaki, mguu, mkate.* So much of what we shared was unspoken, unnamed, beyond language, and yet the new words were important. We were building a house to live in. A house that reflected the sounds and colors and laughter of all our days. A house of words.

Adé made love to me with growing confidence, and I sensed his pride in his newfound skill. After much discussion, one after-

noon we walked to the women's clinic for birth control, holding hands as we navigated the narrow streets. When the young
woman at the clinic informed me of my options — a shot of
Depo-Provera or a shot of Depo-Provera — I remembered reading about the drug; it was used in developing countries as a trial,
to test for potential long-term side effects. It was being tested on
poor women who had few options. Adé said it was my decision.
I focused on the upside of six months without a period, kissed
his cheek, and stretched out on the clinic table. I stared at the
smooth, white, hand-plastered ceiling and, wordlessly, allowed
the long needle to puncture my skin.

THINGS CONTINUED to change.

Adé's cousins told me one day, in the garden, or rather, the patch of grass behind their tiny house, that I should start wearing the *buibui*.

"Not over your face, but your head. You should cover."

They giggled when they said this. It was not an order, but a gentle recommendation to the woman who was to become someone akin to a sister-in-law. I told them it was impossible. I had seen them wrap themselves in the yards of black cloth dozens of times and could not grasp even the most basic mechanics. Silencing me with their insistence and circling me with focus and intention, they showed me how to tuck one corner under my arm, and wrap the other twice around my midsection. Each time the fabric fell to the floor, they laughed hysterically, as if I were the stupidest girl in the world.

"You need one to zip, like an old lady," Maryam said, and they all burst into peals of laughter so loud I was afraid their mother might come and reprimand us.

Enveloped by this bevy of women, I was brought to a shop to buy a ready-made *buibui*. I couldn't understand what they told the shopkeeper, but he took their words very seriously. The women could joke about these matters, but he, a man in a compromised position, privy to the inner sanctum of women and obliged to serve them, could not. He responded to Fatima's requests, her orders, silently and with reverence. He knew their mother, their mother's mother, and their aunts. He knew Nuru and Adé. His father before him had owned the shop. Respect, discretion, and solicitude were the founding principles of his business: as if he were a visitor in their home and not the other way around.

Eventually, we found something suitable — a *buibui* that I could pull over my shoulders like a dress, with a zipper up the front, so that I could, if necessary, step in and out of the sheath without raising my arms. A black scarf wrapped around my head would be worn as a separate piece.

The very next day, Maryam, Mouna, and Sobra ushered me around town in my new garment, introducing me to my new peers: young and newly married women in their early twenties of a certain class — neither rich nor poor, but comfortable, respected, adorned. In short order I learned to recognize them by the movement of their eyes peeking above the strips of black cloth, the way they tossed their gold bangles as they pointed to items in shops, or the color of their beaded slippers peeking from the hems of their *buibui* as they ran errands.

It was the first time Maryam, Mouna, Sobra, and I were able to be together in public. Before then, when I was not covered, I was still outside. It would not have been right for them to be seen with me. On our early trips out, they glided as I stumbled, slowly acclimating myself to the miles of fabric. We walked to the local school and sat at lunchtime chatting with their younger cousins still in attendance. We went to the market together and they showed me which sellers sold the best of each staple. I walked to the beach as one of them now, and leaned against the stone wall with all the other women looking out at the sea, gossiping. The few who spoke English translated my words to the others.

"Ah, she is from *Amrika*. She went to *skuli* there," said Sobra.

Then one of my other future cousins-in-law, usually Maryam, would tell everyone that I was to marry Adé, and all the eyebrows would fly up.

"Kweli?" True?

And she would nod and look at them mischievously, daring them to protest.

"Kabisa," she would say. *I swear.*

Sometimes as they talked, I would sit with my knees to my chest, the hem of my *buibui* grazing the sand. I'd catch words here and there, but mostly I absorbed the women. Their scent was heavy from sweat — the *buibui* was hot (when I wore it, I could barely breathe, let alone ignore the constant stream of sweat that cascaded down the sides of my torso) — and they all wore the same sweet, overpowering jasmine perfume that brought dizzying waves of nausea. A few took the time to speak to and about me with kindness, asking what it was like where I was from, and how I met Adé. Those women told me I was lucky to be marrying him, that all the girls had wanted him since he was a young boy. *So handsome!* they said. *And strong!* A few of them laughed, referring, I think, to his presumed sexual prowess.

Other women were angry and threw cutting knives of jealousy at me with their extraordinarily expressive eyes. The movement of their hands was sharp as they spoke quickly and gestured to me, a newcomer to the circle. I could not understand what they were saying. I wondered if one of these women had been chosen to marry Adé. I could not be sure, but I could imagine the loss of him, and what it might mean to the community — I was a foreigner, after all.

On some days, I felt afraid, neither inside nor outside. But then the breach was always crossed in the tiny room at the top of the hill — on the bed Adé carved, in the world Adé, seemingly, built with his bare hands.

In the evenings, Adé took me to meet the elders — the men and women who raised him, the ones who taught him how to carve, sail, and read the Qur'an. I didn't feel as if he was seeking their approval, but after the fifth or sixth visit, I understood I was being vetted. Each night, Adé would lead me by the hand to a new part of town I did not know existed, with homes secreted behind immense carved wooden doors opening onto proper stone courtyards that to me were as grand as the Taj Majal.

Once inside, it was always the same. Adé would sit quietly in a chair as our host asked him questions about me, my family in the U.S., and our future plans. At Adé's every response, the host looked me over carefully, making mental notes of my features and body movements. I became quite agile at this ritual penetration, and performed the appropriate greeting and leave-takings as required.

None of it bothered me, the strong, independent woman from America. I didn't feel demeaned or degraded. Some would say I could feel this way because I could leave. I still had my father's credit card and my mother's cash. But instead, each meeting brought me closer to Adé. I understood I was his decision. And as each day passed, I grew more confident that he was mine. Why not allow myself to be observed? I had nothing to hide. Why not stand by his side? Was there someone else, anywhere, better than him?

Still, sometimes at night, in our bed, gripped by insecurity, I asked him why he chose me. Because you are my destiny, he might say. But this most often: because you were free to choose, and you chose me.

One morning, Adé told me it was time to visit the *shamba*. I had no idea what this meant, only that we were leaving the island for the first time together, going to the mainland. I dressed carefully. I was not confident enough to wear my *buibui* away from home, but knew I had to approximate the effect, so I put on a black skirt and a white shirt with three-quarter sleeves. I draped my black headscarf around my shoulders, and asked Adé if I looked okay. He pulled the fabric over my head and hair and told me I looked beautiful that way, covered.

"Why won't you cover for me?" he asked. "I am almost your husband, and still you won't cover for me?" And then again, "Ah, but you look like a real Swahili girl that way. Pure."

I laughed and brought it back down, looking into his eyes. We both knew I was not ready. He kissed me then, a long kiss in our little room before a grueling day of travel.

We boarded the ferry. I reached for his hand, but he did not take it, which shocked me, but only for a moment. We were not walking the narrow streets of his tiny town, after all, but entering the larger world of strangers. Within the walls of our room anything was possible. In the island's small village, we were free to roam as young lovers. Away from home, our connection would be maintained through an invisible but unbreakable thread. We would appear separate, but to the trained eye — the people who knew what lovers and husbands and wives looked like in this world — our togetherness would be unmistakable.

We rode the ferry like all the other couples: sitting quietly on the hard wooden seats, looking straight ahead and silently watching the water while the ancient engine groaned. An hour later, we climbed onto the dock and into chaos. I hadn't seen any cars or roads for months, let alone throngs of people arguing and haggling with dozens of street vendors. I had not seen whole groups of people who were not Muslims, who were not Swahili, but Luo and Kikuyu, with round faces and Christian names. I was overwhelmed, but Adé took my elbow and steered me through the maze to a bus stop with an aluminum roof. He motioned for me to sit in the lone empty seat.

Finally, I asked, "*Where* are we going?"

"We are going to the *shamba,*" he said again, meaning the farm, but no kind of farm I had ever known. "We are going to see my father."

My face gave away my surprise. Adé had mentioned his father once or twice, with a quiet detachment that sometimes felt like simmering rage, but more often like a sea of disappointment. I instinctively felt protective. I knew it must have to do with our impending marriage; some unwritten agreement between father and son. I didn't, couldn't, know the depth or the specifics, only that I had to be present, respectful, and strong. I nodded solemnly.

"Don't worry," he said distractedly, "we will not stay long, and we will stop at the house of my cousins on the way back. You will like them. They are three women, living alone without husbands. One of them is studying to be a *daktari.*"

I asked him to tell me more about his cousins. I was always trying to piece together the endless web of relationships, to build the family tree in my mind in order to embed myself within it. But we were already on the bus, and the road had grown dusty and narrow. Adé was withdrawn, staring out the window. We were traveling to meet the father who abandoned his mother for another woman and took no part in raising him. He was seeing the man his mother forced him to respect in the traditional ways, irrespective of his actions. I sensed that my marriage, our marriage, would be the rite that ended the charade. Adé was to become his own man, and this last bit, perhaps a last goodbye, was a crucial exchange.

The *shamba* was a dusty compound at the end of a dusty road that reminded me of the old roads I drove with uncles and aunts in the South when I was a little girl. The dirt was red. Tall grasses grew alongside, suffocated by the dust. I could not picture Nuru living here. It was beneath her, this sweltering heat with no ocean in sight, a barren land isolated from the comings and goings of her family and friends. In fact, I could not see how any of them — not Adé or Amina or Mumin, Adé's brother — would fare without Lamu's narrow stone streets and stately doors, aromatic shops full of chapatis and chai, its sparkling sea at the edge of it all.

Adé flagged the bus driver and we stepped off the bus at an unmarked spot, in a wasteland. I linked my arm into his and he pulled away, growing even more pensive as we walked up the road. I poked his side for levity, but his expression did not change. When we arrived at the mouth of the compound Adé was completely quiet, impossible to read, masked. He had begun to walk a few steps ahead of me as if scouting for land mines, and if any were tripped, he would bear the brunt of the explosion. I wanted to give him support, succor, but Adé was the hero of his own journey now. I smoothed my skirt and felt pride, assuming the role of the young wife-to-be as best I could as we approached the grouping of four small houses, not unlike the shacks where my mother was born, in the South — but these were filthy and run down, and those were not. Five or six children ran, laughing, between them, playing a version of tag. Their clothes were dirty, their houses were dirty, their road was dirty. Adé and I were spotless — the wealthy city mice visiting the poor country mice, except we were not particularly wealthy, just clean and full of hope.

Another turn and then, there he was — Adé's father — on the porch of one of his little houses, sitting stock still on the top step, expecting us, it would seem, with one elbow resting on a raised knee. He saw us, but showed no emotion. He was darker than I had imagined, darker than Adé, than Nuru. He looked hollow, lost, overrun. He seemed angry. He glanced at us, briefly, with a stare so empty that a chill ran through me. It occurred to me that I did not know where I was, or with whom. If anything happened, I would barely know how to get back to Lamu.

Adé made the respectful greeting. "Papa, *shikamoo,* this is Farida."

His father looked briefly at Adé and gave me a quick glance before nodding a begrudging approval. Adé asked after his four wives, and all of their children. He knew all of their names and ages, and each of them came up to him as he spoke and looked at him shyly, with shining eyes, admiration, and not a small bit of awe. He was from far away! He was their big brother, even if they did not know exactly what that meant. Adé pulled small gifts for them out of his shoulder bag, items I had not seen him pack. A *kanga* for the oldest girl, gum and candy for the youngest, pens for the boy in the middle. The wives stood watching without words, nodding their heads in gratitude from doorways. The scene was like an old Western: tumbleweeds, stoicism, unspoken heartache, and an undercurrent of violence.

I wondered if these children had ever seen the ocean. I wondered what it would be like to be related to them. Would they expect me to bring them gifts, to curry favors on their behalf? I respected the family, but knew I did not want this responsibility. Nuru's children would always have my allegiance. But these children did not belong to her or Adé, these children I would not, could not, claim.

After a few more silent moments, Adé pulled out a giant wad of bills — cash I did not know he had, more money than I ever imagined he could have — and handed it over to the wordless, emotionless man. The wives moved closer. The children grew quiet. Adé said something I could not understand, did not need to understand. The money, my presence, his determination to face his father squarely, without deference, were all signs, at least to me, of Adé claiming his freedom. He had been a good son; he had honored his father over the years, despite his father's dishonoring his mother and abandoning him. Now he had his own bride, his own money. He was leaving his father's house.

His father did not count the money, but slipped it into his shirt pocket with a nod. He did not thank Adé, but accepted the bills as if they were owed to him. As if the deal had been struck long ago and there was no need for pretense. Adé paid for his release, and when the transaction was complete, their eyes met and parted for the last time. Adé turned, and I with him, to take our rightful place in another life far, far away.

Adé was quiet all the way back on the bus to the small house in the main town of Malindi, closer to where the ferry docked. The three women — Khadija, Asma, and Halima — his cousins, answered the door with bright smiles and a huge meal of coconut rice and cassava. I exhaled as they spoke Swahili too quickly for me to understand, and wandered through the simple, wood-framed house until I found a room with a small bed. I pulled a few of my *kangas* from my bag for cover, and drifted into a deep sleep filled with dreams of dust, winding roads, and strangers appearing out of tall grasses.

I awoke to darkness and the sounds of the four of them talking in the kitchen under the fluorescent light that shone blue or green, depending on how the light struck the eye. Adé must have told them about me because when I wandered in, they made me a plate of food and started to ask questions about my life in the States. Their concerns were practical, and the sisters communicated with the same straightforward intensity as Nuru had months before. But I was no longer frightened of this way of slicing straight to the heart of things. It was a relief to get to the basics, to know the strength of the foundation before deciding how high a tower, how deep a future, was possible together.

They were especially interested in the details of my parents' divorce. I told them I was still in school and eight years old at the time. My mother had moved to California and my father remained in New York, so I spent my childhood traveling back and forth between them. His cousins nodded knowingly. The splitting of families was not a new phenomenon. Determining the dimensions of the scar tissue was the thing to be done.

"How far was your mother's house from your father's?" Asma asked. "From Malindi to Lamu, or Malindi to Nairobi?"

"No, no," I said, searching for a closer parallel. "More like Nairobi to Saudia," using the same shortened version of Saudi Arabia that I had heard so often at Nuru's house when they were discussing the ultimate pilgrimage — making the hajj.

"*Ohhhh,*" said the three of them almost at once, while looking at me with pity. "*Far.*" Khadija ran her hands over her kanga, punctuating her assessment of the damage.

Later that night, in the bigger bed they had given us, Adé told me more about the women. Halima had mental problems and would never marry, he said. These troubles had been with her "since she was a little girl and her father wanted nothing to do with her." She was being taken care of by the other two, both sisters by different fathers. Khadija was studying to become a doctor — "not an ordinary doctor but one who helps people who have problems in their heads, who cannot understand things as they are." And Asma, the one with the chocolate skin who laughed at my stuttering Swahili, was "to be married to a man in a high position" and would always be known as the one who married so-and-so, with a name of prominence and respect. From then on, it would be as if the entire family had married this man, because that is how it was in Swahili culture. I did not ask what kind of high position. Politics, religion, it meant the same: she would have more power as his wife, which would elevate the power of all of us.

In the morning, the sisters asked me what I thought of Adé's father and I made a face, opening my eyes wide and raising my hands as if to say I could make neither heads nor tails of him. They looked at each other, and laughed.

"He is not a good man," Khadija said.

"Adé is the best that came out of that one!" Asma agreed. "He will not dare come to the *harussi*. Nuru would not allow it."

And then they laughed and laughed, and I laughed along with them because I knew Nuru too, and she would never tolerate her ex-husband's presence. The image of any attempt he would make to show up despite her wishes was comical, absurd. But Adé did not laugh as we did; he chastised us.

"He is my father. It is not right for you to speak of him this way."

Halima turned her head away from where he sat, as if his voice were coming from somewhere else.

"You will never have to see him again," Asma said. "You have given him money even though it is he who should have given it you, or is it? He has seen Farida is healthy enough to have children. You will have your own family now. He cannot ask anything else of you. It is over, *basi*."

Adé was quiet. She was right. There was nothing more to say.

ON THE DAY we returned to the island, a heated discussion was taking place in the small causeway of Nuru's house about the absence of my parents. Amina translated the main points for me, and told me that after marathon sessions late into the night it had come down to the issue of parental approval. Permission to marry must be granted in person. Adé had to approach both of my parents in the traditional way and ask if our families could be joined. If my parents agreed, money would be exchanged.

This I could not understand. "My parents are to give you a dowry?" I asked Adé as we listened to Amina's recounting.

"No," Adé said. "My family is supposed to give *your* family a sum of money to put away for the things we will need after the wedding — plates, furniture, clothes, silver — whatever we need to set up house. The money is a seal. Once paid, plans for the *harussi* can commence because your parents will know that I can take care of you, and our future children. My mother is very concerned about all this. Will your parents come to Lamu, or should I go to *Amrika?*"

I didn't know what to say.

"You have to understand, Farida," Amina said. "The coming together of the families cannot be avoided. The *harussi* is for them too. By the end of the ceremonies the two households come together as one."

A few of the women slapped their palms together as if to say, *yes*, that is it — the thing that cannot be sacrificed. The others grew quiet, nodding. The *harussi* would be impossible without the involvement of my parents.

There was also the issue of my personal, bodily ablutions. Only women were allowed to discuss these matters and a dozen came to Nuru's house the next day for just that purpose. Flinging off their *buibuis* at the threshold, they seated themselves on cushions around the edges of the hallway, with their backs against the wall. I sat with Adé's grandmother on her raised wooden cot, feeling exposed, as if my naked body was being prodded like a mango for tenderness. But I was also happy, because this was another sign of belonging: what happened to me mattered.

Again, Amina translated the salient points for me. It was unusual but not unheard of for Swahili men to marry women from the West, but Adé was special to the community and so customs must be observed as faithfully as possible. A son like Adé was not simply thrown to the wind.

At the moment the women were discussing the *singo* that should be applied in the days leading up the wedding, a purifying paste of jasmine, rose petals, sandalwood, and other ingredients Amina struggled to translate.

I nodded, and then thought of my own parents. They would ask if I loved Adé, if he made me happy, and once this was determined, my father would quietly assess Adé's net worth and calculate his ability to provide for me. My mother would embrace Adé, and immediately move on to his mother and the other women in the family, eventually setting up shop on the floor among them.

Adé's family was different, the assessments more carefully calibrated. Many of the women were adamant that my own mother be responsible for the bridal rituals: taking care to bathe and dress and present me in the right way, to ensure I had a respectable number of gold bangles on my wrists, and to provide monies for food for the days and days of feasting. Everyone seemed to agree on this, but then Nuru stated the obvious: my parents were unable to complete the tasks. Even if they came for the wedding, they did not know how to prepare me in the traditional way.

After much back and forth, which Amina mercifully did not translate, an older woman, her eyes ringed with kohl, spoke while gesturing passionately with her hands, as if scripting a solution in the air. This time, Amina translated: Adé's cousins would apply my *singo* and the elaborate henna designs that would cover my hands and arms, and Nuru would take charge of the many fittings for the vestments I would wear at various stages of the weeklong celebration. Another cousin would arrange for the preparation of the all-important chicken biryani.

Meanwhile, Adé was having his own meetings with men of the old town. One night after one of these assemblies, we were pressed against each other in the darkness of our narrow bed and he said abruptly, "I tried to talk and find a way around this, but it is true that I must go to your country and ask your parents for permission to marry you. The imam says this is the only way it will be allowed."

I raised my head to face him. "The *only* way?"

"It is for your safety, and also mine," Adé said. "Your parents will still have the right to reject me if we marry without their consent, and to give their full and true consent they must see my face."

I sputtered. Of course my parents would agree, sight unseen, I said. They trusted me. I knew my own mind. I was not a child. I could make my own decisions. I wanted to marry him, and that would be enough for them.

He shook his head. "It will not work, *mpenzi*. We will not be married any other way."

I had never heard Adé concede an impediment, nor had I, until that moment, imagined in any detail the looming cultural collision: Adé in my father's office on Madison Avenue, or the apartment on the Upper East Side. Adé, who had never been in an elevator, never seen an escalator, never been on a plane. My father would find his approach antiquated, and brush it off. *If you make my daughter happy, of course you can marry her. That is all that matters.* My father would then take us to lunch at the steakhouse across the street, clearing a path for us through the beer-drinking, gray-suited Wall Street guys, the likes of which Adé had never seen.

Family dinner would be torturous. My stepmother would ask Adé about his island, nodding politely as he attempted to describe the intricacies of woodcarving and his hyper-extended family. She would pretend to understand and take great pains to mute her judgment about the multiple wives and tens of cousins. She had never breached the continental divide; for all she knew Lamu was a rural Harlem. But later, in the privacy of their floor to ceiling beige bedroom, she would ask my father if her grandchildto-be could ask the four questions at Seder if he was part Muslim. My father wouldn't know and would wonder out loud, as he took off his socks and stretched his pale feet, how Adé could make it through life without a glass of white wine every now and then.

My mother would be easier. I could take him to her house in Northern California, and settle into one of the small structures that resembled our room in the old town. She would stream African music — from West Africa, not East, where Adé was from, but African all the same — through speakers, and offer her future son-in-law a meal of collard greens, cornbread, and fresh roasted chicken. She would tell Adé the greens had come from her garden, and after dinner take his hand and lead him through her large house. She would show him the Native American arrowheads and African baskets she collected before introducing him to the sauna.

Adé would not be able to speak until after the tour. My mother would light the already laid fire in the great stone fireplace in her living room, and settle into the enormous brown cushions of her custom-made couch. Moments later, she would listen with great solemnity as Adé asked permission to marry me. In return, she would deliver a perfectly balanced, ideologically informed response.

"Ah, of course the two of you can marry. But it is not up to me. You will learn this if you haven't already: my daughter is very independent, which is how she was raised. She does not need anyone's permission to love. She is free."

And Adé would nod, but think her bizarre, incomprehensible.

Later, walking the path to our little house on the property, he would ask, "Don't your parents care who you marry? Don't they care about my family? Or what your life will be like in the future?" Then he would stop, turn to me, and say, "We will not be that way with our daughters."

"No," I would say. "We will not." And then I would kiss him full on the mouth, on the hillside, under the moon.

ONCE I ACCEPTED the necessity of the journey home, the trick was how to accomplish it. Suddenly, the reality of President Moi and the police state began to factor more prominently in our family conversations. First, Adé needed a passport, and for that we would have to go to Nairobi. He would be the only one in the family to have the little blue book, and only if we were lucky and bribed the right official with the right amount of money at the right time. As we mapped out our route, it occurred to me that Adé had never seen Nairobi and neither had most of his family. I tried to comprehend this, how people could limit their movement to such a tiny area — an island and two small coastal towns — no matter how sprawling and chaotic. And then we started hearing the stories. One of Adé's cousins had been trying to get to Saudi Arabia for twenty years and disallowed fourteen times.

An uncle threw up his hands. "He was trying to make the hajj, to Mecca, and they blocked him even from this!"

Even Adé's stepsister, the oldest daughter of Nuru's husband, was punished for trying to leave the country to go to secondary school in Tanzania — raped by a government official who promised her a passport in return.

The stories were awful, but I did not think they held any particular relevance for us. I was American. I would be with him and speak to the official in charge. The passport would be approved. If not we would go to the American Embassy and I would meet with someone in an air-conditioned room. I would explain, and they would agree to help me within a few hours. I thought it might take two days, maybe three, for the paperwork to be processed, but no one seemed to believe me. I had long forgotten the hundreds, maybe even thousands of posters of the president plastered all over the city. The relief Miriam and I felt once we were far from Moi's piercing eyes.

One night in bed, already exhausted from the endless planning, I asked Adé if he thought our plan was too dangerous. The timing seemed inopportune. Many people said Moi's government was near collapse, and each day brought newspaper reports on government soldiers attacking peaceful protestors calling for democratic elections. Members of Parliament were disappearing, or found dead. By now I had seen it too — the tribalism Adé often mentioned. In the months I had been on the island, several Swahili had lost their jobs to men from the Kikuyu tribe, relatives once or twice or three times removed from the president.

"Ah no, of course not," Adé said, as if we had our own special tunnel to the other side of trouble. "It is fine. We will succeed. I will meet your parents, and then it will be finished."

Adé showed no special interest in travel itself; his preference was only for me. His acceptance of our mission was complete; travel, with all of its risks and rewards, was now a part of his life forever. His biggest concern was for me. When we traveled together, I would be seen as Kenyan, he reminded me again and again in the days leading up to our departure. From the people this would mean familiarity: easy conversation and a total disregard for my personal space; from the police, it would mean disdain and a cold inhumanity.

"The police work for the government," he said. "And the government wants us all to be afraid so we will not push for elections, so we will not control our own future. If you were *mzungu* it would all be very nice, *Yes madam, no madam.* But if they think you are Kenyan, they will keep you from standing up. I feel sorry for my country. But it will not always be like this. Things cannot stay the same forever."

I nodded, but did not, could not, comprehend the reality. From my sheltered American perch, I imagined checks and balances, the rights of the individual, and judicial protection, even though history had shown me otherwise. In the town where I was born, Jackson, Mississippi, whole police departments were run by violent white supremacists, by the Ku Klux Klan. When I was a child the Klan threatened my parents for "stirring up trouble" by pushing for integration, but in my family mythology, my parents had fought back and won. That was the American way. I could not imagine defeat.

The next morning, Nuru walked us to the boat, drawing her black scarf over her face so that only her eyes could be seen. She watched us climb aboard the creaking ferry with tears in her eyes, the three of us sober with the gravity of the journey ahead. We were leaving all that was safe — the familiar streets of the old town, the protection of Adé's sprawling family, and our room at the top of the hill, with its perfect, unobstructed view of the sea.

MY EDUCATION BEGAN almost immediately on the bus from the coast to the capital. One minute the long, narrow machine was careening over the dividing line and back, and the next, we were hurtling through the darkness in the middle of the night. And then a giant spotlight shown through the giant windshield, and men in uniform waved the driver to the side of the road. Many of the passengers were unmoved by the change in momentum, but most woke up quickly, their eyes becoming alert once they heard the police yelling at the driver. He jumped out as directed and was pushed to the side.

By now, we were all sitting up, eerily still. Adé and I had shifted and twisted our necks to see what was happening, and brought ourselves to full attention as a team of soldiers boarded the old shell of a bus. They were noisy and demanding, lumbering through the center aisle, banging on seats, barking orders, and pulling down bundles from overhead racks. The soldiers had guns — Ml6s or AK-47s or Kalashnikovs, I couldn't tell — slung over their shoulders, and as they rummaged through the sacks, pocketed yards of cloth and handfuls of fruit, smiling when they found small stashes of money or bangles of gold. Before I could stop myself, I demanded, in English, that the soldiers stop. Adé tried to hold me back but my outrage was instinctual. People were losing what was likely their life savings, the result of months if not years of labor. My reaction was natural, inbred, and inviolate.

And then I felt the barrel of a gun against my cheek — cold, hard, and terrifying. I had leapt from my seat, and one of the soldiers grabbed me. He pressed his large hand around my mouth and moved his body so that the butt of the gun would make contact with my face. It occurred to me that if the gun fired, the bullet would exit through the top of my head and lodge itself in the aluminum roof of the bus. As if in a dream, I imagined the metal passing through me, and relinquished my resistance. I felt the silent, potent awareness of my fellow passengers, watching the scene unfold. Most had seen or heard about *kitu* like this: things that happened on the night bus to Nairobi.

The soldier turned me away from Adé, but I sought his eyes anyway, and then heard his voice, composed as always. Adé spoke quickly in Swahili, calming the soldier, explaining, apologizing, and somehow managing to keep his dignity at the same time. He knew the tone had to be perfect, a sign of desperation might cause the soldiers to become drunk on their own power, but humble logic might remind them that indeed there was someone or something more powerful to reckon with, a higher authority beyond their control.

I let my body go slack until finally the soldier threw me back into my battered seat where I remained, looking up at Adé in disbelief as he sank back down next to me and wrapped his long, protective arms around my shoulders. The soldiers took everything of value and jumped off jauntily when they were finished, tapping the side of the bus and telling the driver to move on. As the bus made it over the slight curb from the shoulder and back onto the road, the passengers stood to check their things and assess what was lost. I went into what I suppose was a kind of shock, and stayed awake for the next six hours fighting catatonia. Adé's arms were warm, but I was not. I stared out the window into the black night, waiting for a glimpse of daylight that might reveal the familiar shapes of things — trees, buildings, the road itself.

Adé tried to reassure me before falling asleep. "It is over. That is it, they are gone."

But for me it was not so easy. Something inside of me had shattered, and I could not put the pieces back together so quickly. I did not think, as I imagined Miriam would have, that I had just experienced "the real Africa." I thought instead that Adé was only the king of his tiny island, which meant that the farther we traveled away from it, the less likely I was to be his queen. The shift from powerful to powerless rocked me to the core. It was not a position I wanted to inhabit. I did not find it redemptive or romantic. I was not titillated by danger. For the first time since I arrived on the continent, I felt dread. I saw myself as a foreigner, an interloper in a struggle that was not my own. I had my first pang of homesickness. Then I felt like a coward, and tried to wave it away. *It was normal. I am fine. We are fine.* But it didn't work. The seed had been planted.

When the sun finally rose, Adé stirred in his seat, and asked if I was okay. I nodded, stroked his hand, and leaned over to kiss his mouth. But I had lost our words.

IN THE MORNING we arrived to the familiar, incessant bustle of the city, the frenetic energy that had sent me to the island in the first place. I could tell Adé was enthralled by the tall buildings, fancy cars, and restaurants on every street, but he took everything in with cool detachment. He intuitively understood his innocence could be exploited, that he could be seen as an easy target for someone looking for a mark. He revealed his giddy excitement only after we had arrived safely at the hotel, the tiny stack of rooms Miriam and I found the year before. After I handed my credit card to the man behind the desk, he gave me a key and pointed to the tiny metal box that was to take us up. Adé eyed the elevator quietly, but once inside, it began its slow ascent, and his eyes widened. He jumped up and down to feel the jerking of the carriage. He smiled at me then, a huge, happy smile, like a child discovering a long-coveted toy, too long hidden inside wrapping paper. He leaned over and planted a wet kiss on my cheek.

"I have never been in an elevator," he said, thrilled.

"I know, *mpenzi*," I said, laughing. "I know."

We lay in our rented room all day, recovering from the bus ride beneath threadbare blue blankets, making love, pressing hard against each other to stave off the wicked chill. It had been so hot when Miriam and I were here, I was not expecting such a drop in temperature, and yet there it was, again, the unpredictable.

At exactly six the next morning we prepared methodically, almost ceremoniously, for what lay ahead. I wrapped the colorful, embroidered money belt Miriam had brought me from Thailand around my waist and covered it with the modest white shirt I had worn to the *shamba*. I paired it with a long black skirt I had made in Lamu, hoping my modesty would telegraph synchronicity with the sober Christianity that dominated this inland city. Adé velcroed his identification papers, stashed in a waterproof, plastic sandwich bag, inside a beige zippered pouch we had bought especially for the trip, around his ankle.

By seven thirty we had taken our breakfast of toast and juice from the tiny buffet in the hotel basement, and set off for the American Express office in the nicer part of town. I redeemed five hundred dollars of my dwindling funds in U.S. currency, tossed a thick packet of letters Miriam had left for me into my bag without a thought of their contents, and then we headed for the passport office. Adé was determined to arrive early. He did not want to be the first in line because he thought that would attract too much attention, but he wanted, at the same time, to get it over with.

Others had the same idea, but from the moment we entered the huge processing room in the innocuous city building and confronted the bleak row of cubicles, each manned by — Adé told me — a member of President Moi's tribe, it was clear by the way the workers all raised their heads and glanced at me, looking me over, trying to read me, that my presence meant something, though neither of us could determine what, and whether it would help or harm. The bus ride flashed through my mind. No matter how hard I pressed the reset button, I could still feel the butt of the gun against my cheek. The debilitating powerlessness. And I could not stop thinking that by staying in this country, I would be subjecting myself to such treatment by choice.

The eyes of other Kenyans bore into me as we waited for hours in the line of blank, expressionless faces fanning themselves with their meticulously filled out forms. A few other Americans sat on backpacks, standing every few minutes to move up in line. They joked with each other and shook their heads at the interminable wait but remained relaxed. I should have felt an affinity with them, but I didn't. We did not share the same fear. They had not been on the bus.

Finally, we arrived at one of several identical desks and spilled out our story, only to be directed to another line and made to wait again for "the person in charge of passports and visas" as opposed to only "passports." Then the office broke for lunch, during which brightly colored plastic thermoses and little balls of cloth-wrapped food appeared on desks, and workers merrily swapped jokes and told stories.

At last we met Mugo, the short, sturdy-looking official with warm eyes assigned to our case. My first thought: a piece of cake. But then I noticed Mugo's body language as Adé spoke to him in Swahili and explained our intentions, the way he leaned back in his chair and took stock of us. I saw contempt slide across his eyes. He was older than Adé; he thought Adé disrespectful. The smug downturn at the sides of his mouth suggested that he found Adé's tribe beneath him. He pressed his lips together in anger. Adé had won an opportunity to leave the country. Once Adé received his passport, he would be in another class, one that soared above Mugo's. At some point, Mugo realized that he would have to stop his mind before it went off the rails, and he abruptly cut Adé off with a wave of his hand. He responded in English, looking at me as if Adé had said nothing at all, and reached into his desk for a thick stack of papers. "Fill them out," he said, "and come back in three days." He would speak to us then.

I swallowed my fear and stepped boldly forward — the money of the operation. I assumed the position and reached into my wallet for one of the crisp twenty-dollar bills I had requested from American Express. I lay a twenty on top of the stack. I was deferential, but also jocular. We all knew I was speaking in shorthand. Was there someone else in the office that could process the forms more quickly? He looked down at the money and laughed.

"Ah, so you are familiar with the way things work here, I see. No ordinary *mʐungu*. You have been here for some time."

I jumped at the chance for camaraderie. "Yes, yes, I know how it goes. We take care of each other, *au vipi?*"

Adé nudged me from behind when I said those last words and a current ran between us. *Au vipi* was a Swahili phrase that Adé had taught me, a phrase we used often because it summed everything up so well. *Au vipi? Isn't it? Isn't it true? Isn't that right?* At first, Adé used it after explaining something to me. Like why a son should always take care of his mother, or why I should let his friend Abu Bakar walk me to the store at night.

"Because if you go to the store alone, Farida," he said, "the men will look at you and wonder why you are alone, and they will think you are free, like any other woman from America. But if Bakar is with you, they will know he is taking you for me because everyone knows Bakar is my friend, and so it is the same as you and I going to the store together, even though I am here taking care of my grandmother. You will be safe then, *au vipi?*"

Isn't that right? Do you understand?

In turn, I added *au vipi* to my repertoire of seduction. I would move over Adé's body in our little room and rub against him saying, "This feels good to you, *au vipi?*" And he would look up at me sheepishly and smile his shy, excited, private smile at me, his first lover. "You want me now," I would say, "*au vipi?* Are you ready for me, *au vipi?* You want me to do this, *au vipi?*" And he would nod, yes, yes, yes. I want. I want. I want. And I would throw back my head and laugh, and then every other time he said *au vipi,* we both laughed because it had this other meaning, too. It meant we wanted each other and had our own language for it. It meant there was another truth.

I put down another twenty as Mugo considered my question, and then he took the money. "Fill out these forms and come back tomorrow," he said, still avoiding Adé's gaze. "I will see what can be done."

We started walking back to our room, the daunting forms tucked into my shoulder bag. I noticed the crisp blue sky and riotous bougainvillea dotting the city for the first time. I told Adé it reminded me of San Francisco, one of the places where I grew up, and hoped we would soon see together. I put on my most optimistic face and said I thought things had gone reasonably well, considering everything we'd heard before leaving the island. Adé did not agree. He said that the people of Mugo's tribe looked down on the people from the coast. It had always been that way, he said. They believed in their churches. They did not believe in the Prophet Mohammed. They thought Swahili people were stupid, backward. That Swahili people thought they were better because their skin was lighter and they kept to themselves. And now the Kikuyu had all the power, and could do with it what they wished. It was simple; it was devastating.

He was quiet. I wagered it would take two weeks. He bet me two months.

We stopped for food in the restaurant of a hotel for tourists and expats — several of whom were reading the *International Herald Tribune*. I craned my neck for glimpses of the headlines, and saw a notice that my president was seeking a "Push on Operation Persian Gulf," and then turned my attention back to Adé, who was studying the menu with irritated befuddlement. I looked down at the laminated page. Shrimp cocktail. Club sandwiches. Banana daiquiris. I hadn't had a sip of alcohol, let alone seen dozens of bottles of it, for weeks, but here the bar took up one whole wall of the dining room. Adé did not believe in even sitting so close to the stuff, but I could tell he was trying, for me, for us, for the future.

I ordered hamburgers and fries — there was no fish, or rice, or greens of any kind — an orange Fanta for him, and a virgin mint julep for me in an ironic nod to the stinking realities of colonialism. I chuckled as I ordered, but Adé did not, and I did not have the energy to explain the joke, the reference to plantations, to slavery. Instead, I brought out the forms and read them as we waited for the food. They were in English, which I found deplorable, and there were dozens of questions. They wanted the names and addresses of the brothers and sisters of each of Adé's parents, along with the names and contact information of all of Adé's schoolteachers from primary school onward, as well as all of his employers. If the applicant owned his own business, how had he raised funds to start it? Whom did it serve? If it was a business for tourists, did the applicant have the proper license from such and such bureau at such and such address? If not, it would have to be acquired before the passport application would be considered.

For each question we would have to leave unanswered, I tallied a twenty-dollar bill. By the time the food arrived, the total exceeded seven hundred dollars.

Adé was no stranger to hamburgers and fries, but after weeks of lentils, coconut rice, and cassava, we could barely digest the meat, and fell into our narrow bed back at the hotel as if drugged. Adé fell asleep immediately, but I lay there in the dark, thinking of Mugo, and the long line of bodies we would encounter the next day. I turned on the light and pulled out the papers. I tried to make headway, but there were too many questions I could not answer. When I lay back down, Adé instinctively reached his arm around me and pulled me closer. I wrapped my legs around his, and nuzzled my face in his neck, inhaling deeply. My faith had suffered a blow, but my love for him, my devotion, remained.

Hours later I woke up ravenous and dressed quickly. I craved eggs, the slick white outer oval and pasty yolk inside, the symbol of life hidden inside the protein-rich orb. I wanted these and maybe some juice — mango, papaya, something orange and *tamu*, sweet. Adé, who usually slept so lightly and seemed always ready to spring into the day, was unmoving in the metal bed, his long body wrapped tightly between the thin sheets shielding him from the cold of Nairobi's altitude.

Downstairs the desk was unmanned, but I didn't notice the

aberration. The streets were deathly still, but even that didn't register in my First World mind. I blithely walked the recently swept street from the hotel down to a shop I knew, and found it shuttered. I kept walking until I found another, similarly pad-locked and impenetrable. Then I came to a corner where I had seen vegetable stands the evening before, but there was no one and nothing in sight, not even a remnant of one of the crudely constructed stalls, or a dirty orange peel left on the ground. As if in a dream, I wondered if I were the only living person left on Earth. Where were the voices and movement of other souls, the music blaring from the *matatus*, the screeching of worn tires on even more worn asphalt?

And then I felt, without hearing, the rumble of trucks, and then all at once they were upon me, real and monstrously loud. Columns and columns of tanks were rolling through the city. They were gigantic and immediately served at least one of their purposes, which was to make me feel small — very, very small, in-consequential. I could be crushed with one turn of the wheel as if my life, our lives, and everyone we brought with us, our mothers and fathers and their mothers and fathers, and all the mothers and fathers before them, were meaningless, not even a full entry in the annals of humankind.

Instead of running, which would have been futile, I stopped moving and became my own pounding heart. Sweat streamed from my armpits like urine. Soldiers were perched on top of the tanks, and hung from the sides like components of the machines themselves. Huge guns were strapped to their bodies, ammuni-tion sashed over their hearts, red berets atop their heads, their dark faces inscrutable but for the flash of excitement in a few grinning mouths anticipating the kill. As each tank passed me, I was assessed and dismissed, held in the sightline of a weapon, caught, then released. This happened thirty or thirty-five times.

I held my breath, counting the steps back to Adé, and carefully charting the path in my mind. But then a boy stepped out of the shadows of a dilapidated building across the street with columns left behind by the English. He had on short pants, a ripped T-shirt with a faded Coca-Cola logo, and worn-out tennis shoes — the kind travelers often leave behind or give away before returning home, where new shoes could be bought easily and cheap. He started running, but the shoes were a few sizes too big and slowed his progress. He could not have been more than twelve or thirteen years old. The soldiers yelled at him in English, then Swahili, and then in a language I did not recognize. When he did not respond but kept on running, one of the mechanized men pulled the trigger. I watched the boy fall to the ground. I was the only other person on the street. The shooter tilted his gun to me, the witness, as his tank drove by. I wanted to vomit.

When I began to breathe again, I did not know what to do. I felt the butt of the gun against my cheek, and knew better than to cross the street. The tanks had passed. The boy was dead, bleeding out on the sidewalk. I made my way slowly back to our room, and found Adé waiting anxiously.

I walked in, and he jumped up. His face was overcome with fear. Where had I been? Another guest at the hotel, a Dutchman, had told him about the protests at the university. Troops had been sent in to quell the "disturbance." I should *not* have been on the streets, he said, should *not* have left without him. I nodded and told him, shaking, about the boy, and he folded me into his arms

and held me, again. I felt all of his concern, but also a creeping numbness. I could not imagine a day when Adé would turn
against me, but I could, for the first time, imagine something far
worse: death, imprisonment, or cruelty at the hands of a foreign
government. Dictatorship and secreted civil wars created a ter-
rible isolation for the people who lived within their unfolding. I
saw a hideous and surreal picture of reality with no escape. Adé
would not mistreat me, but I had not considered the state. And
suddenly I felt less than I had yesterday, and far less than I had
the week before. I was losing something. I was going dark.

ALMOST A THOUSAND dollars and three calls home to both of my parents for more cash later, Mugo finally told us that Adé would get his passport. We could pick it up, he said, in six weeks. Relief flooded our bodies, and we ran almost immediately to the train station. We could get to the blue hills without a passport, and see the Great Rift Valley from beds that folded down from the sides of a deluxe passenger car. We could find the Ngorongoro Crater and see buffalo and giraffes. We could go to the Serengeti and look out at the arid plains. We could even get to Arusha and Zanzibar, the island of spices, without a passport. We could leave Mugo and the dead boy on the street.

But the sound of the shot followed me. It was freezing inside the crater, and we had no clothes to keep us warm inside the tent we rented on the rim. It was startlingly beautiful, but we had no words and no warmth to express the majesty of what we saw. The Maasai were there, too, standing in groups and perpetual time-lessness, staring at us but speaking only when I began buying their beaded jewelry, and even then, we did not understand each other. I ended up with bags of their creations — necklaces, belts, and pendants for friends back home — only to find a few days after we left the crater that none of it could be worn. The smell of cow dung permeated the beads and the wire on which they were strung. The reddish grease the Maasai smeared on their bodies stained everything it touched. By the time we crossed over into Tanzania, I had to let go of all the beautiful jewelry because I could no longer breathe with it in my bag or on my body. I did not want to throw it away, so I left pieces of it at bus stops and restaurants, a sack of earrings on the train.

In Arusha, we searched for hours to find a guide who would take us into the Serengeti for the least amount of money. We found a man named Daniel, who was keen to talk to anyone who might listen to his story. His father had died and made him chief, but he did not want to be chief. Of his village or town or tribe I did not know, but I couldn't blame him. In his jeans and T-shirt and cowboy hat, he looked frightfully out of place. Adé and I whispered about his plight as we counted our shillings. Was Daniel mentally unstable, or telling the truth?

Later, Daniel told us he wanted to be a writer. He had written a novel and wanted me to read it. There were poems in his pocket, dozens of them. He read a few of them aloud as the safari jeep trucked alongside enormous giraffes, and crouched near lions who looked at us with so little interest I wondered if they even saw us sitting before them. Were lions able to see human beings, or did they have some form of human-blindness?

And then again: the shot. I was standing up in the jeep as we bounced alongside hundreds of flamingoes when I took another bullet, this time to the head. The steel plate that opened the roof of the jeep, the thing that gave it a giant eye, had not been secured properly. We hit a bump and up it flew, a square piece of solid

steel, knocking me to black. I lost some moments and then returned, the strong, sturdy American, insisting I was fine. Daniel
was beside himself with worry. There was me, and there was also
his lack of insurance and his not wanting to be chief and the potential failure of his attempt to be something other than chief. It
was all very complex for him.

For us, it was less so. I was fine, but needed to lie down. We
could not afford a room at the fancy lodge in the heart of the Serengeti, but Daniel's uncle worked there so we drove up, the uncle
was located, and he showed us to an empty room used by workers who sometimes stayed at the lodge for months at a time. I slept.
When I woke, my jaw hurt. I asked for aspirin, the kind in packets
that mix into water and juice like sugar, the only type I could find
since I arrived in Kenya. Adé found them for sale at the gift shop.
He asked how many I wanted. I said ten, a dozen, two dozen, a lot.

Adé decided that Daniel had "the same kind of trouble as
Halima," which meant he was unstable, *kabisa,* not just lonely.
We wondered again if Daniel was ever named chief of anything.
Did his father even die? Adé said that sometimes families "threw
children with mental problems away." Maybe Daniel was one of
those. I could not be decisive, but Adé was clear. He stroked my
arm tenderly as I massaged the side of my face and jawbone. I
loved the animals, especially the giraffes, with their graceful but
awkward lope, but it was time to move on. We needed to get back
to the water, to the sound of the call to prayer. We needed to be in
our *kangas* and *kikois,* where things were simple and known. We
left for the coast, and another island. Zanzibar.

I called home a week after we arrived on the new but reassur-
ingly familiar island, to hear concern in my father's voice. Where

had I been and why hadn't I called in such a long time? I told him everything and nothing. The passport was in the works, and we had seen lions. The man I was to marry, my fiancé, was eating chapatis and drinking a cup of steaming, clove-rich chai. We had found a house by the ocean to stay in until the passport was ready. The man who owned the house said if Adé helped him paint the exterior, we could live there for free as long as we wanted.

I loved everything about the Zanzibar house — its lack of electricity, and the roar of the ocean just outside our window at night. It was at the end of a long road, and stood alone. Mugo's glare, the image of his hand palming the succession of twenty-dollar bills, began to fade. The pain in my jaw subsided. I still heard the shot, but more faintly. Adé heard nothing but the sound of moving forward. Rice and *mchicha* sustained us, and so did the sun. It was hot in the day, blinding, then breezy and warm at night. The air was thick. Women wrapped rich blue pieces of indigo around their waists, and the conch shells tumbled from the sea like watermelons: huge, smooth, heavy. I picked them up when I walked along the beach at low tide, and rubbed their smooth hardness against my cheeks. One night, his hand on my belly, his face in my neck, Adé said that he wanted children, lots of children, and I laughed and said that I did, too, but only with him, always with him. In that house I remembered again why I was going to marry Adé. He was my future.

And then our time was up; the passport must be ready, it was time to go. We fell asleep that last night in the double hammock outside our bedroom door. The next morning Adé woke up perfectly rested, but I was covered with huge mosquito bites so red they looked like targets.

The shot, this time, a bite.

MUGO DELIVERED ON his promise, or we got what we paid for, I couldn't tell which, but the little booklet emblazoned with Adé's name and picture was now safely tucked inside our suitcase, its blank pages waiting to be filled with the stamps of other, more exotic, gatekeepers. We had done the impossible. We had vanquished all comers. In Nairobi, a travel agent told me about a flight from Mombasa to New York with only one stop in Frankfurt. The plan now was to go home to see Nuru and Amina and Mumin and Aliyah, and everyone else whom we knew were waiting on Lamu, breathlessly, no doubt, for our safe return. We would proclaim our victory before flying across two continents and at least one vast ocean.

We took the morning bus out of Nairobi. I remember that the seats were red, and the windows covered in dust. We sat with a bag of oranges and a few cold Fantas. As the bus pulled out of the crumbling bus station, I rested my head on Adé's shoulder and fell asleep. When I opened my eyes, I sensed the bus was moving too fast. A dull ache at the back of my head made me squint. My right eye twitched. I began rubbing my jaw. Adé saw the signs and brought out a little packet of aspirin to mix with the Fanta, but by the time we reached Malindi, my headache was so brutal, so relentless, so devastating that I could not stand up. I told Adé in a whisper that I could not walk off the bus. He helped me to the door, but when it came time to step down I fell, and the sea of people waiting for loved ones and friends all moved to the side so that Adé could catch me, hold me, anything to keep me from tumbling to the ground.

There was shouting. One of Adé's relatives appeared from nowhere, a cousin of his cousin, and the two of them walked me, one arm around each shoulder, my feet dragging, to a small house that let clean, inexpensive rooms. The man at the desk looked at me without emotion, judged the factors and pointed us to a room on the same floor. I collapsed into a bed with a green blanket. I felt Adé's hand on my forehead, and heard the worry in his voice. He went to find a doctor, and left me alone in the room. The faint glow of the fluorescent lights in the hallway shone through the translucent glass of the transom above the door. I heard footsteps and a man's voice calling a few times, but that was all. I trusted Adé, but I was also beyond fear. My bones were too heavy to care.

He came back with news that a doctor was coming to the hotel. This was unusual, but Adé had arranged it. We were back in his realm. When he spoke, things happened. Another cold stethoscope, more talking that I couldn't understand. Then a blood heat rose in my forearms and began creeping slowly to my neck. I tried to get up, but the dizziness got the better of me. Adé's cousin said his mother could boil the herbs used to treat malaria. The doctor said I should go to the local *hospitali;* I was too sick for herbs. He said it could be malaria, or something worse. I felt the heat spread across my face: first my cheeks, then my ears. My feet tingled. A pain was coming on in my lower back. I looked at Adé and he looked at me, and the cousin looked at Adé, and Adé looked at the doctor. Then Adé started moving quickly, faster than I had ever seen him move before. He opened our bags and pulled out my *kangas* and toothbrush. He took my passport, shillings, traveler's checks, and my sole credit card, and put them in the pouch around his ankle.

"It's time to go to the hospital, *mpenzi*. I am going to find someone who can drive us. It is only a few miles. Not far."

I nodded, turned my head to the side, and threw up all over the floor.

I could not walk. The light of day was like a dagger to my eyes. As we negotiated passageways, I felt people staring, asking what was wrong with me. Was I sick, drugged? Were the men helping me decent or not? Adé spoke to them quickly in Swahili as we progressed through successive challenges: the narrow hall, the slick steps, the closed doors, the crowded sidewalk, the broken handle of the car door, the seemingly endless drive, the haggled fare to the hospital on the outskirts of town.

And then finally, it was over. We had arrived. The effort it took to get up the steps to the entrance of the small one-story cement building was monstrous. The one nurse we found, holding forth behind a giant slab of counter like a butcher, looked as if she might be related to Mugo. She wore a huge cross around her neck, and I thought that she, too, might have to be bribed. She glared at me with the same disdain and superiority that we'd grown accustomed to in Nairobi, and spoke in English, my language, not Adé's or, for that matter, her own.

"What are you bringing her here for? You know we don't

have rooms here for *mzungu*." I was the foreigner. And she was a relative of someone in the government. Things would not go smoothly.

Adé responded bitingly, in Swahili, shaming her into doing the right thing. We weren't in Nairobi, he said, reminding her that it was she, not him, who was the minority in this town. The nurse sucked her teeth and slapped down a clipboard with forms. When he shifted his hip just the slightest bit to try and pick it up, I slipped from his arms and onto the floor. My kneecaps absorbed the fall. Sweat dripped off my chest. There were flies.

"Malaria, something else maybe," she said, peering over the counter. "So how you going to be covering this cost? You her sugar daddy or what?"

Adé reached for my wallet and pulled out the credit card.

"We don't take that here, you know. You're going to have to find cash money." She rubbed her fingers together. "Paper."

I felt Adé growing angry. He began demanding things of her, but I lost track of what he was saying. His words were becoming muffled, as if I were hearing them from the bottom of a bright, blue pool. I saw the white of the nurse's uniform, and the green and yellow leaves on the bushes outside the window. And then I let go.

I did not grab hold again until two days later, when I opened my eyes to see a nurse walking toward me with a needle she had just used on a patient lying inert in the bed next to mine. The row of beds beyond looked to be at least ten patients deep. I was alone. I located my belongings — a black shirt, my little embroidered bag — resting on a chair next to the bed. I was no longer on fire with fever, but my neck felt as if it were in a cast. I could not right it; I could not look at the ceiling. Even the soft light of dusk coming through the slatted window coverings hurt my eyes. The nurse caught me searching for Adé.

"He's not here. He said to tell you if you woke up that he'd be coming right back with food. He's been waiting here for hours and hours, but once he saw what you'd be eating, he ran back to his cousin's house to get you a proper plate of mash."

I nodded as best I could. Tried to move the tongue in my mouth that felt as thick as five garden slugs, and equally dumb.

"The needle," I managed. "What's in it, and you've used it once already. Can I have a new one?" I looked at her, hoping for kindness. "Please?"

She shot me a glare. "Americans always worried about the needles, but we clean them. Didn't you see me run the saline solution through after I gave the last injection?"

I asked again, this time to see a new sealed package and the needle coming out of it.

The nurse laughed at me and then started talking to herself. "This girl is about to die, and she's worried about the needle. Unbelievable. She thinks because she's in Africa she's going to get AIDS from one of our needles, isn't it?" She stood over me and jabbed the many-times-used steel point into my shoulder. "Dr. Simba is coming in the morning. You can talk to him about the needles, if you don't like how we are taking care of business."

I felt the liquid displacing what was already there, the blood beneath the skin. If I could have moved my arm, I would have immediately rubbed the spot where the needle had punctured me, but I couldn't lift my limbs. I felt like an amputee. Where were my legs? Why couldn't I turn my head? I thought perhaps there was a brace around my neck, but I could not reach up to check. I watched the nurse go from bed to bed, taking temperatures, administering injections with the same needle, holding a little cup of juice for each patient who was swallowing pills. I could barely make them out, but I could tell the other patients were thin, gaunt, hunched. Their affliction all carried the same affect, a kind of downward pull, and I wondered if they had malaria, or whatever it was that I had, too, and if I looked like them.

The medicine left a metallic taste in my mouth, and I felt my eyes closing. That same sense of going underwater, of leaving that place, descended upon me. I woke up at noon the next day to Adé rubbing my forehead and reading poems in my ear. He had found *The Captain's Verses* in my bag. I smiled at his face, his beautiful, open, loving face. And I rested my cheek in the cup of his hand.

"Hello, *mpenzi*," he said, continuing in our half-English, half-Swahili language. "You are safe, don't worry. My mother cannot come because it is too far for her and she has the children to look after, but I am here. Khadija is cooking for you. She is making all of your favorites. Are you hungry? I have here some *mchicha* with coconut rice."

I tried to get up onto one elbow and fell back down. I didn't feel hungry, I felt empty. But I needed Adé to feed me again. I needed to know I was still alive. I took the forkful of rice he offered into my mouth, and then, things began to change yet again. I loved Adé, but I could not understand this hospital. What was I doing there, what was wrong with the other patients? How had I gone from sweet spaghetti and our little room at the top of the town, to a place that felt like a holding cell for the dead and dying? I heard Miriam's voice in my head. *The real Africa.*

I knew there was no such thing, and yet. Perhaps this is what she wanted all along. The Africa she saw on television, where people were poor and naked and hungry and dying of AIDS. Where we Westerners, stripped of the niceties and conveniences we took for granted — like new needles and private hospital rooms — would have to live by sheer will. In the real Africa, we would have to wake from our lazy slumber and shake off our ignorance born of so-called privilege. We would have to grasp the nettle of our raw, human potential and respond to the uncertainties of life. But again: I was not interested in such a mission.

I looked at Adé, extending the fork again and again, whispering encouragements, and I saw, for the first time, not a stranger, but a person from another place, another world. I saw someone I loved but could never fully know. Adé knew how to talk murderers out of pulling the trigger. His father had abandoned him and his mother for four other wives and twice as many children. His island did not have a hospital. He made his living with precise movements of his hands and knowledge of the sky, chiseling flowers into wood for the rich, and knowing the direction of the wind as he steered his dhow. He lived in a house with no electricity and no running water, and shoveled feces from the bathroom — the hole in the ground at the back of his mother's house — every month. Five times a day Adé washed his hands and arms, knelt on a beautiful rug, and prayed to an invisible God.

But it was more than this. Yes, I could see it now. It wasn't him, it was *me*. I had done what I swore I would not do: *I* had romanticized Africa. I had accepted Adé's life before I realized what it might mean for my own.

Three weeks later, the worst was over. The chaotic storm had miraculously let me down with no permanent bodily harm, but the undertow was moving in quickly. Chloroquine had been pumped through my veins for so long that everything tasted bitter; the metallic taste of it invaded my mouth, my lungs, my everything. The fever had cooked my body so thoroughly that every pore was wrung clean from the burning.

Adé had made friends with everyone in the hospital by then, and I knew it was probably those friendships that had saved my life. The hospital had almost no resources, and was full of people dying of incurable diseases, but Adé had made sure they gave me clean needles. Three nurses tended thirty patients, but my bedding was changed every day. Food came to me like clockwork in little tins wrapped in cloth. Dr. Simba was rarely available, but I was told he checked my blood daily to chart the activity of parasites. I had cerebral malaria and a rare meningitis. I needed ongoing treatment, treatment I could only get in America, but I was getting better.

In my newfound moments of coherence, my eyes found Adé sitting in the chair beside my bed, and he would make me laugh by reminding me of all the silly things I did, like saying *au vipi* to Mugo. Soon he began giving me tidbits of news: Amina had given birth to a baby girl. His brother Mumin had been accepted to the University of Nairobi. Nuru was praying for my recovery.

And then a few days before I was due to be discharged, I was stronger and the news grew more serious. Saddam Hussein had invaded Kuwait. The United Nations had levied sanctions against Iraq. All cargo going in and out of that country was suspended. And now there was a no-fly zone over all of north and east Africa — especially the coast where we were — because it was predominantly Muslim. I had to get home, but all commercial flights had been cancelled indefinitely.

Adé shifted in his seat, his normally sunny face a mask of gray, and explained slowly, carefully, as if recounting a story from long ago, that my family had been calling for daily updates and he'd called them back, pouring coin after coin into a pay phone in town. They had been trying to cut through the chaos since he first told them I was in the hospital. My father was devastated by the news but, having seen tragedy, sprang into action, reaching out to powerful clients, friends, relatives. Strings were pulled and favors called in. And then, just that morning, Adé received a call from the American Embassy in Nairobi. A special plane had been arranged and it would come to get me the next day at one o'clock. I would need to take the ferry to Lamu in the morning, and then wait for the plane to land on the island's tiny airstrip. It would be on the ground for twenty minutes. If I missed the window, I would not be able to leave for weeks, perhaps months. I might die.

Here, Adé paused. "Farida," he said. "There is something else." He looked up and I could see, for the first time, in the weeks of him caring for me, that he had aged. He was no longer the boy who had never been to the city, no longer the young man who believed that life could be better, freer, somewhere else. He had met me, and left his island to find a harsher, less forgiving world. He looked at me and held my gaze, holding me as best he could for the impact.

"There is only one seat on the plane."

And then the bullet blew a hole straight through me.

I LEFT THE hospital that afternoon and the nurses watched, wondering, I am sure, how it would all play out. Adé and I had become a spectacle, a couple in one of the Bollywood films the people of Malindi loved so much. Our love was exotic, tragic, destined; each incident in our story propelled the movie along. Adé gathered my few belongings and the bag of medicine that Dr. Simba had prepared for the journey. I nodded as the doctor signed the release and ordered me to check into a hospital as soon as I arrived in New York. The parasites were aggressive, and I would need to be monitored. I nodded again, and glanced back once more at the giant room where I had spent the worst weeks of my life. My bed was stripped; all traces of me, of Adé sitting by my bed feeding me coconut rice, were gone.

The nurse called a taxi and Adé lowered me gently into it, telling the driver not to rush, that his wife was still weak. His wife. It was the first time he had said it. We looked at each other, resolute, as he slid into the seat beside me and took my hand. The driver slowly navigated the narrow streets in the old town of Malindi and I became acutely aware that we would shortly be spending our last night together. I ran my hand over his again

and again, trying to memorize the length of each finger, the depth
of each crease, the contours of each patch of softness. I stared
out the window at the men heading home for evening prayer, at
the groups of women in their *buibui* walking, the sun setting behind them a deep orange. I breathed deeply, as if I could inhale
the whole world with him in it, and grasped Adé's hand a little
tighter before pressing my forehead against the windowpane between me and the dusty chaos, the faded stone facades, and the
promise of a future I had thought was mine.

When we arrived at his cousins' house, Khadija was cooking
mango soup. Asma walked me over to the bed to show me how
she had covered it with a breathtaking piece of silk-and-cotton
fabric, a precious piece of blues and browns, no doubt pulled
from her marriage trunk. I sat on the bed with big cotton pillows
behind me, and Halima came to lay her head in my lap. We sat
there for a long time, me stroking her hair as she sobbed, telling
her it was going to be all right.

Adé entered the room with my medicine and a glass of water shortly after dinner. I had managed a few bites from the huge
tin tray Khadija had placed before me, but the effort had been ex-
hausting. Adé could see it in the way I moved, and quietly asked
if he should pack my suitcase. We both checked the clock, gaug-
ing the time before we slipped beneath the beautiful bedspread
for the night. It was nine o'clock. The ferry left at eleven the next
morning. I nodded, and Adé pulled my suitcase out from under
the bed. At that moment, an extraordinary alertness came over
me and I became very still. I didn't want to miss anything, as if
the tenderness infusing his every movement was important and
true and the summation of everything, and my only purpose now

was to bear witness. I could see he was trying hard not to cry as he folded my red and purple *kangas* and gingerly gathered my gauzy undergarments. He was attending to me as if to a precious child, his devotion a wish for everything to be easy, even as I was preparing to leave.

It occurred to me that I was the girl from America who taught him that the country on the other side of the ocean was not so far away. He was the Swahili boy who taught me how to find joy in limitations, and showed me that home was not a physical place, but something much larger and more mysterious. Adé's love meant that even if I could not bridge the entire world, the gaps of my life were not insurmountable. I was lovable, complete, just as I was. Another me, an unbroken me, was possible. As I watched, part of me wished that he would take control and tie me to a bed-post in the middle of the room — anything to make me miss the plane. But Adé was not looking up. He was not reading my eyes. If he did, he would see that even though he thought this was now our fate, one of us could try, at least, to put a stop to it.

But Adé believed that life was held together by law. He could still apply a Swahili saying or *sura* from the Qur'an to any heart-ache with precision. And yet I could see that our time together had taught him that words could not always protect him, that he, like many others he'd never truly fathomed, could suffer a blow from which he might not recover. This recognition had not hit me, for I did not yet have an understanding of all that I'd be leaving behind. I did not yet know that in leaving Adé, I was not just leaving him, I was leaving everyone who loved him, whom I had also come to love. I would probably never see Nuru, or any of the people I had come to think of as family, again.

And so, while we held each other through the night, I reassured him. I will be back, my love. There is nothing to fear. It will only be a little while. I just have to get well and do some arranging, and then we'll be together again. I stroked his back, and went on and on about our future: when I would return, when he would visit me, when I would call, at what phone, at what hour, how we would struggle through the static to reassure each other of our love. He had bought postcards, dozens of them, and given me half, each one with an address written neatly in the designated square. He would have bought stamps, he told me, but I would have to get them in America. I smiled at him, at his thoughtfulness, the way he remembered every detail, the way he knew how to love in this complete way, conscious of it all, and yet rising to act with optimism in the face of all that appeared futile.

It was a long night, with Adé's body high above and inside of me, a night of heat and loss, ecstatic exclamations, and desperate cries of mourning. And when we peeled ourselves away, I could feel the tissue of our fresh new love tearing in two.

Adé woke me up at eight with a kiss on my forehead and when I opened my eyes, I was terrified.

"Khadija has made breakfast for us," he said softly.

I struggled to raise myself from the bed and stumbled, but Adé righted me and, together, we made our way to the kitchen. Halima was staring vacantly at her plate. Asma was gone, I did not ask where. I could barely taste the food. Toast with jam and butter. Hard-boiled eggs. I ate for strength, but nothing else.

The rest of the morning was a blur, perhaps because the whole time I was wiping tears from his eyes, or Adé was wiping them from mine. The first two hours were a farce; we kept bumping into each other as we tried to move through space and time as discrete bodies, each of its own volition. We had been together for months, day after day, night after night, and by the end, I rarely left the house without him. When he wasn't working or sitting with his mother, he was with me — cooking, eating, talking, laughing, joking, making love. How would this separation work? We breathed the same air. Our bodies had changed shape to fit each other. I had never been so close to anyone in my life. Where would he go after the plane took off? What would he tell his mother and sisters? The imam? Would I be the cause of shame, disappointment, anger?

Khadija insisted we stand outside the house for photographs. She pulled out a small, inexpensive camera and pressed a passing neighbor to capture the moment, to preserve the memory of our almost family. In the photo, I am wearing a white-and-black-striped shirt with my long black skirt. My skin is pale, and my eyes squint at the camera lens. My arms are wrapped around Adé's waist, and Khadija's arms are wrapped around my shoulders, and Halima's arms around Adé's. Asma came running up from nowhere moments before the neighbor pushed the button. She knelt in the middle of us, her arms spread wide, her smile irreverent.

THE PLANE TOUCHED down on the tarmac at one o'clock exactly. Adé and I were waiting on the black tar in the hot sun, surrounded by my bags from Malindi. There was no time to get back to our little room on the hill for the rest of my things. Adé said he would send them, or keep them safe until my return. The plane was larger than I had imagined, but decidedly full. Adé walked me over, but a man in uniform blocked him from escorting me onto the plane. Adé tried to tell him I was sick, that I could not carry my own bags, and promised he would get off the plane immediately, but the man was wearing headphones, and shouted back, "No time! No time!" The whole scene reminded me of *Apocalypse Now*, which made me cling even more tightly to Adé. Finally, the man ran down the steps to where we were standing and began to pull me, physically, away. But Adé did not let me go. Instead he whispered to me and stroked my back and told me I had changed his life completely, and he would have no other love. He told me to tell my mother and father that he would meet them soon, and he would write his first letter to me that night and send it in the morning.

He said it was time for me to let go. It was time to get on the plane. I needed to be home, where my family could take care of me, and I would get well. I told him he was my family. Kiss Nuru for me. And Amina's baby. He said he would, but it was time to go. He wiped the tears as they fell and kissed my cheek and told me there was nothing more to say. Our house of words is on the inside now, he said. The rest was in the hands of Allah.

I boarded the plane and sat down quickly, straining my head to find Adé through the window. I could see him searching for me in each one. Then the door closed and the engine started. The blast of air from the air conditioner hit my face, cold and artificial. The plane started to taxi, and then he saw me. I lay my palm flat against the window, and he nodded, raising his hand to meet mine. And then the gathering of speed, the roar of the engine, and the nose of the plane reared up. Adé was meant to fly, I thought, and I felt like a goose shot from the sky, but not with me.

I looked down at the island and in place of Adé there were now many islands: the archipelago. Briefly I wondered what other lands he would see without me, where his new passport would carry him, as if it was obvious from the start that this is how it would end. That I would have to leave Adé where I had found him, love's perfection, no more and no less than the blossoming of a seed.

Two decades later, I have forgiven myself for leaving, for trying, for dreaming, for all of it. We burned brightly, and then the rumblings began. Now I have only gratitude. For him, for us, for that place in time when I relished the long, bumpy ride on the truck from the old town loaded with cassava and cardamom. Our days together marked me for life. In Adé's sturdy embrace, against all odds, I had learned the meaning of home.

I veiled for him, and he peeled me open each night, unwrapping my sarongs, my brightly colored scarves, one at a time, as the flame of the white candle by our bedside flickered hungrily. Those days at the end of the world gave me a taste of freedom. I did not have to perform a self. We, who moved as one, were already aching. We walked for miles on the shore at low tide, our feet burning until we found the wetness of the sea, fell into her cooling waters, and emerged renewed, the white of his teeth meeting the whites of my eyes.

Twenty years ago we lived by the sea in a small green house that you painted every year after the rains. Do you remember, *mpenzi?* And in that house we made love almost every day, and dreamed about all the lands we would see together, and in that house I imagined writing a book about being there with you. The book would be about love. I knew that then. It would be about living deliriously without all the things and people I held dear. I had you and I had the sea and I had the beautiful blue indigo the women wore on the cloths wrapped around their waists. I had fish and I had the taste of you — salty, musky amber. *Do you remember?* I do.

Because I remember everything.

Acknowledgments

I thank everyone.

Made in the USA
Columbia, SC
09 January 2023

75699621R00079